OUR
HEALING
BIRTHRIGHT

OUR
HEALING
BIRTHRIGHT

Taking Responsibility for Ourselves and Our Planet

ANDREW M. CORT, D.C.

Healing Arts Press
Rochester, Vermont

Healing Arts Press
One Park Street
Rochester, Vermont 05767

LIBRARY OF CONGRESS CATALOGING IN PUBLICATION DATA

Cort, Andrew M.
    Our healing birthright: taking responsibility for ourselves and
our planet / Andrew M. Cort.
      p.   cm.
    Includes bibliographical referencs.
    ISBN 0-89281-376-8:
    1. Holistic medicine. 2. Health. 3. Ecology. I. Title.
R733.C67   1990
613 – dc20   90-33683
                                        CIP

Printed and bound in the United States

10 9 8 7 6 5 4 3 2 1

Healing Arts Press is a division of Inner Traditions International, Ltd.

Distributed to the book trade in Canada by Book Center, Inc., Montreal, Quebec

Distributed to the health food trade in Canada by Alive Books, Toronto and Vancouver

Peanuts cartoon reprinted on page 92 by permission of United Feature Syndicate, Inc.

For Marjorie Spalding

Contents

Acknowledgments

No book can be written, revised, and produced without the help of many people. For her help with the content and editing, I especially want to thank my friend Marjorie Spalding, who read every draft, and who patiently put up with my slowness and stubbornness in taking her advice—which I eventually always did. Eighteen years ago, it was Marjorie's influence that initially aroused my interest in the healing arts, so this book is dedicated to her for both of these reasons.

I also received many useful suggestions from my sister, Barbara Counter, Ph.D., and from Robert Appelbaum, Carol Binswanger, Raymond Brown, M.D., Michael Ellner, Naomi Trier, and my parents, Robert and Stella Cort.

Chapter 2 owes a special word of thanks for all I have learned from my fellow board members of H.E.A.L. (Health Education AIDS Liaison), as well as to the many extraordinary men and women who attend our Wednesday night meetings.

For their help with computers and word processors, all of which was foreign to me when I began, I want to thank Julian Lines, Peggy Ford-Fyffe, Dennis Grecco, Paul Reiss, Stephen Helfand, Charles Wright, Karen Karavanic, Don Mermelstein, and most especially my late friend Bruce Ford-Fyffe.

Several people were helpful in efforts to bring this book to the attention of a publisher. I want to thank Terry Barry; Lyn Familant; Ron Lavine, D.C.; David Rosengarten; Mark and Susan Black; Robert Lawlor; Joscelyn Godwin; Ted Kaptchuk, O.M.D.; Frank Lipman, M.D.; Nick Bamforth; Elizabeth Dugger; and, of course, my editor at Inner Traditions, Leslie Colket.

Finally, a great many people helped me with this effort in ways I can barely begin to acknowledge or repay. These include my patients, various colleagues, and some remarkable friends and Teachers. I respectfully offer this book to them.

Preface

Pick up any book that discusses "holistic health," and you will read that the first consideration in health care must be prevention. But I have a strange secret to reveal: There is no such thing as prevention.

Prevention would mean not allowing yourself to become unhealthy to begin with. Health, contrary to its usual definition as the absence of pain and symptoms, means that every organ and system in your body, every cell, every process, every thought, and every emotion, are all functioning perfectly. Health is not just the absence of disease, nor is it the opposite of disease. Health is a state of optimal well-being. In today's world of high stress, fast foods, and polluted environments, none of us can claim to be in such a state. We are long past any consideration of prevention. What we need, what we *all* need, is *healing*.

Healing is not just a matter of eating bran flakes. Nor is it solely a matter of jogging, taking medicinal drugs, popping vitamins, or finding the right guru. There is no quick-fix gimmick.

No one wishes there were one more than I do. For almost twenty years I have shared this body with two chronic, aggravating illnesses. I have tried just about everything offered in medicine, chiropractic, acupuncture, homeopathy, herbs, meditation techniques, counseling, and nutrition. In the course of this search my personal experience has been that although I have not been cured entirely, each of these systems has had a significant contribution to make, and I remain in much better health than the original prognosis would have suggested.

All of this has taught me that health is a much larger and deeper issue for all of us than simply finding "the" thing that can make us feel relatively okay. Listening to my patients during my seven years in practice, and watching such statistics as the overall national increase in cancer, arthritis, and heart disease, I have become convinced that people are living longer but becoming less healthy—and that they (and I) want to know why this is the case and what we can do about it.

The answers are not simple. As I say, no one would appreciate a simple answer more than I would. But that is just not possible. We are physical, sexual, emotional, psychological, social, and spiritual beings. To be truly healthy, all of these aspects of our beings must be functioning perfectly in themselves, and in a balanced relationship with each other. And for all our impressive and sophisticated modern knowledge, it remains true that we still have much to learn about our bodies, about our sexuality, about our hearts and minds, about our society and civilization, and about our souls.

Thus armed with an incomplete understanding of ourselves, of each other, and of our world, we face the most terrifying of times. We do not know whether we shall destroy ourselves first with crime, pollution, economic collapse, racial war, AIDS, or a nuclear holocaust. In the face of all this pending horror, our tendency is *not* to fight for our lives with every reasonable and heroic effort we can muster: our tendency is to numb ourselves with television, drugs, pornography, and gossip (and to ignore the reasonable and the heroic, because they seem either too boring or too naive, or both).

There are two questions at issue in this book. The first, stated most simply, is: What is health? This question has to do with the nature and cause of disease, the methods of treatment, and the overall aims of the individual. It is a matter of great debate among health practitioners and patients alike. The second issue is the question of our responsibility to our own health, to each other's health, and to the planet's health. Because if I should ever finally overcome my own health problems, and even go on to become totally, optimally, and gloriously healthy, while the whole world goes to hell around me, then I have done nothing very important. Personal salvation by itself is a fantasy masquerading as an accomplishment.

Healing is an ongoing quest for balance and self-perfection. To help us attain this, the marketplace is filled with books and articles telling us what to do. But all the fragmented information available to us—the various suggestions on nutrition and exercise, the various types of treatments, the various psychological techniques—has become unwieldy and confusing. We need a way to simplify this diverse and conflicting information into one coherent perspective, so that we can take steps to improve our health with complete confidence in what we are doing. For that reason, in the following pages, I present a simple unified theory of healing based on the age-old understanding of the threefold nature of the universe. It is my wish that the reader will use this perspective, and all the practical information the book supplies, as a sensible guide for achieving the highest possible level of wellness.

Since this is a book about threefoldedness, it is only appropriate that I should have two more wishes for the book's success. My second wish is that you will find that some parts of it challenge your attitudes and beliefs. I hope that the *ideas* in the book will allow you—as they have allowed me—to think in new ways about health, science, and responsibility. This is as good a time as any for me to confess, with gratitude, that the vast majority of ideas on these pages, certainly all the important ones, are not mine. Finer minds than mine discovered them. For myself, and for my own overall healing process, I just try to understand them. If I have failed to do so, or if I have stated them poorly, of course, the blame is mine alone.

The earth supplies us with food, the sun supplies us with energy: a state of constant giving. Yet a law of nature says that for every action there must be an equal and opposite reaction. If something is given, according to this law, then something must be gotten in return. Nothing is "free." Everything costs something. Does this include life itself? Could it be that we have some unknown obligation to the earth? Perhaps even to the sun, or to the universe at large? And might this be a better question for science to ponder, rather than seeking new ways to conquer nature?

When health care is concerned only with combating disease and symptoms, it allows us to engage in the dangerous illusion that we can keep doing everything wrong (to ourselves, to each other, to the planet) and that we will somehow "get away with it." As long as scientists find a cure for heart disease, we can keep on eating badly. As long as scientists find a cure for cancer, we can continue to pollute the environment. But everything in this universe must be paid for. Nobody "gets away" with anything. Because we do not remember this, we have given ourselves over to a cycle of self-destruction and mass destruction. The incidence of heart disease is *rising*. The incidence of cancer is *rising*. Waiting for a magical cure is a deadly mistake. Waiting for a magical invention to save us from a nuclear holocaust, while we continue to stockpile nuclear weapons, is the very same deadly mistake on an even more terrifying level. We make this mistake on *many* levels. We look for something for nothing. We forget that we have to pay. We must now take the responsibility for changing the situation we are in, and it has to begin with changing the way we *think*.

A final wish I have for this book is that it will make some people angry. Not angry in the sense of spitefulness or violence, but angry in the sense of a passionate outrage over the endless and insane poisoning of our food, water, and air, and the continuing threats to destroy one anothers' lives. We all know that this is happening. We have to ask ourselves why it is so hard to *feel* anything much about it, and why we rarely bother to *do* anything about it. This may be the most important question for our times. Just as there can be no excuse for the destruction of the planet, there can be no excuse for apathy. In part, this book is my small way of taking a stand against the greed, ignorance, destructiveness, and self-destructiveness that together are leading us quietly toward our own death. I hope to make you angry and concerned enough to take the same stand, and to take effective action.

Introduction

Why do some people get sick, while others break all the rules and still remain healthy? Is there one best system of treatment? Why do certain measures help one patient, yet fail with another? Why do some things come back, some never go away, and others just go away for good by themselves?

THE CAUSE OF DISEASE

Orthodox medicine has traditionally said that a germ causes disease, or that some poison causes disease. Holistic healers traditionally say that something in the patient's habits or status (e.g., poor nutrition, a misaligned spine, lack of exercise, etc.) causes disease. Psychologists claim that something in the patient's mind or emotions causes disease. Psychics claim that something in the patient's spirit or past actions (karma) causes disease.

All of these explanations are wrong, because they are all incomplete. No one thing is ever responsible for any disease. Rather, three factors can be seen as simultaneously necessary in every case.[1] There must be an *active cause*, a *receptive cause*, and a *conciliatory cause*.

The Active Cause

Something unnatural and potentially damaging must *act* on the body. For instance, this might be a bacteria, a virus, a poison,

radiation, an environmental pollutant, a minor injury, a carcinogenic chemical, and so forth.

But such elements are almost ceaselessly in contact with our
bodies and environment, yet we do not all continually fall sick
en masse. So there has to be some additional cause (unless you
want to go with blind luck, and there is too much evidence
against this).

The Receptive Cause

Something in the body must be already out of balance and thus
receptive to being abnormally acted upon. For instance, this
might be a liver weakened by poor nutrition or alcoholism, a
congenitally weak heart, or any tissue that has been overwhelmed by the degenerative effects of stress. Under the best of
conditions, the body is designed so that an occasional invading
germ or poison is harmless. But deteriorated tissue is fertile
ground for disease.

Even so, nature has provided us with massive disease-
controlling abilities. If an abnormal, "sick" process begins in the
body, our immune system is designed to marshal extraordinary
forces for fighting off the invaders and repairing any damage.
Our nervous system, blood supply, and hormonal system are
designed for rapid communication and defense. In other words,
even if some damaging active agent should begin harming some
unsound receptive tissue, our normal healing forces should
quickly put a stop to it. If they do not, then there must also be a
third factor involved.

The Conciliatory Cause

Something in the total man or woman, against all of nature's best
intentions, must inappropriately allow the sickness to take hold
and persist; it must allow the active agent to continue damaging
the receptive body. This "something" is usually most perceptible
as a run-down immune system (although the full extent of nature's healing force is larger by far). As we shall see later on, the

strength of our immunity is a joint function of physical, emotional, psychological, and spiritual factors.

This is why not all cigarette smokers get lung cancer. Cigarette smoke *is* a carcinogen, and it is surely foolhardy to dare our body and psyche to handle this unnecessary carcinogen. But if a particular smoker was born with a "good constitution," if he eats well, exercises, and takes care of his health in most ways, then he may get away with the smoking by not giving the carcinogen any weak tissue to act upon. Again, if he has a truly healthy emotional and psychological life, then his immune system may simply not allow the cigarette smoke to react lethally with his body.

Some people never get sick when they visit a sick friend. Some people smoke, drink too much, have lousy diets, never exercise—and never get sick. Some people are always angry, depressed, nasty—and physically healthy. This is because *all three factors must connect* for the body to go careening off into disease; one or even two of the factors alone will never be sufficient.

Looking at this from the opposite perspective, some people are warm, loving, even happy-go-lucky, and do get cancer. Some people jog and eat plenty of salad, and still have heart attacks. Things are not as simple as we would like them to be; it is all a matter of proportion and blending of the three simultaneous causes. That outwardly happy-go-lucky fellow may be repressing an inner negativity that he is not even aware of. That jogging salad-eater may be living with a genetic abnormality that no amount of healthy habits can completely overcome. And it goes without saying that a massive dose of poison or a horribly virulent germ may sometimes overwhelm any of us, no matter how well we care for our body, mind, and emotions. Still, although it is possible for one or another of the factors to be overwhelmingly at fault, we see that (in variable proportions) all three factors are always involved in every disease. In Part 1, we will look at the particular circumstances of contemporary life that enhance these three factors and lead to the pervasive illnesses of our times.

Balance is the normal aim of a healthy body. Every bodily process, when left untampered with, tends toward a state of balance. In physiology, this dynamic tendency toward balance is described by the word *homeostasis*. (It is interesting to observe that emotional, psychological, and social "balance" apparently require our conscious effort, whereas the physical body and the physical universe will self-regulate toward balance so long as nothing interferes with normal functioning.) Physical illness can always be seen as involving a loss of balance, which results in some part of the body losing its normal relationship with the body as a whole. For instance, the body may produce too many cells (cancer) or too little insulin (diabetes), or may suffer from too much blood pressure, too little vitamin A, or some other imbalance in energy, chemistry, or physiology.

THE PROCESS OF HEALING

As disease is a threefold movement toward destruction, so healing is a threefold movement toward repair. In disease, a dangerous agent was allowed to act upon an unbalanced body, throwing it further and further into imbalance. For healing to take place, the same internal force that previously allowed the disease must now become the active healing force, and must actively work to restore a state of balance. The tissues of the body must become receptive to this force, and the total person (body, heart, and mind) must now allow and encourage the process of restoration.

The Active Force

A force for repair must become active. In other words, the body must start doing its job again to repair the damage. This process *may* be enhanced by outside help in the form of some sort of healing remedy or healing technique. In its least substantial form, such a remedy will simply try artificially to replace or oppose the body's own forces for a short while. Sometimes this is necessary. This is the purpose of most medicinal drugs. In its highest form, the remedy will serve to redirect the body's forces, to nudge the body itself back into appropriate action. Either way, the actual healing is something we do not understand: only the body itself knows how to do it. (See chapter 3 for a discussion of mankind's many efforts to stimulate the active force of healing.)

The Receptive Force

Meanwhile, the damaged, unbalanced tissue must now become receptive to these healing activities. For instance, if a germ was able to damage some part of the body because the proper nutrients were not present to preserve the tissue's strength, then those nutrients must return so that the tissue itself no longer presents an "obstacle" to healing, but becomes receptive to it. Here is where good basic health habits are necessary, including good nutrition, appropriate exercise, proper breathing, and relaxation. If our physical bodies are so badly cared for as to be unreceptive to healing, then no medicine, no technique, no remedy, and no amount of happiness will help. (See chapter 4 for a discussion of the simplest ways to encourage and maintain a healthy, receptive body.)

The Conciliatory Force

Finally, in order for the active healing force to be capable of repairing the damaged but receptive tissue, the total person must be in a state in which the overwhelming tendency is in the direction of life and health. The state of our psyche, through its powerful interventions in the cardiovascular, endocrine, nervous, and immune systems, provides the third healing force that either reconciles a poisonous substance and weak tissue to disease, or reconciles a healing action and strong tissue to health. The whole man, the whole woman – body, mind, and emotions – must be passionately dedicated to the aim of reclaiming our natural birthright. This third factor is the most important consideration in any attempt to fuse a complete triad of successful healing, and it is the one to which we are most likely to pay the least attention. (In chapter 5 I discuss the enhancement of this third healing force by means of meditation or visualization techniques or by changing our thoughts, feelings, and attitudes.)

Put most simply, the aim of healing is to restore lost balance. The body has a nearly overwhelming tendency to do this by itself. If something is interfering with this homeostatic tendency, or if something has caused the body to fall so far out of balance that it can no longer correct itself without help, then it is possible (and occasionally necessary) for a doctor, or other healing-arts practitioner, to be of use in the process of reestablishing normal balance. But to do this it must always be remembered and respected that the body has its own powerful, innate, instinctive intelligence. If the body is trusted, and an attempt is made to understand it, then a doctor can be of genuine service to the healing process. But if any part of the body's awesome intelligence is ignored or thwarted (which is what we usually try to do), then further imbalance must sooner or later ensue.

In fact, if any part of the whole person is not taken into account – which is what happens when we think we can separate our mind and emotions from our body – then some degree of sickness is inevitable.

And this leads me directly to the second theme of the book, which will be discussed in the final three chapters. We have seen that the holistic approach is not simply a vague idea: it is an integrated, coherent, threefold way of thinking and an effective, comprehensive, threefold way of acting. In terms of personal healing, holism rejects the expectation that someone outside ourself should prescribe that one simple thing designed to cure our various ills, as if an illness were somehow isolated from the rest of our existence. In terms of planetary healing, it similarly rejects the expectation that the right program, law, or policy, by itself, is all we need to transform the world. Rather, the threefold approach of holism is equally applicable to social change and to physical change. And we shall see that this harmonious, cohesive perspective, unlike the fragmented technological perspective we usually apply to our health and our politics, is the only serious way to bring about any genuine, lasting change.

There is nothing metaphysical or metaphorical in the idea that no one can become healthy all alone. Just as an individual cell and each individual thought will affect the overall balance of the entire human body, so each individual human being has a dynamic and irrevocable effect on the overall balance of the environment and the human community. Healing is never just a personal matter. Sickness anywhere is a threat to health everywhere.[2]

PART 1

TRENDS IN
CONTEMPORARY ILLNESS

Generally speaking, most medical statistics today seem to indicate that the age of infectious diseases is behind us. Our friends and loved ones are not dying of smallpox, polio, measles, or tuberculosis. Antibiotics, vaccines, and improved sanitation have apparently changed all that. (In fact, one of the reasons why AIDS is so frightening to so many of us is that it is a throwback to something we thought we were rid of: a plague, a viciously infectious disease that threatens to destroy everyone on earth. AIDS is a fluke, an exception; it does not fit the pattern of modern life. I will return to this important topic in chapter 2.)

Today we are primarily confronted by the following triad of illnesses:

1. Cardiovascular diseases (such as heart attacks and strokes)
2. Chronic inflammatory diseases (such as arthritis and colitis)
3. Cancer

Note that none of these are infectious diseases, caused by some arbitrary microbe from an external, hostile nature. We do not avoid heart attack victims for fear of catching coronary artery disease. Nor do we avoid arthritics or victims of lung cancer for fear of picking up their germs. Although germs may sometimes become involved in these disease processes (as nature's scavengers, microbes are supposed to eliminate old, sick tissue), they are not primary factors. No, ours are diseases of deterioration, diseases in which the body itself is doing something wrong. It is still possible to improve this situation, and the first step is to gain a clear understanding of exactly what is happening to our health.

1

Modern Diseases Have Their Reasons

Cardiovascular diseases, chronic inflammatory diseases, and cancer are very much interrelated, and all three are the inevitable result of three particular contemporary circumstances: excessive stress, poor nutrition, and environmental pollution. As we shall see, these three factors supply us with an abundance of active, receptive, and conciliatory causes for the various pervasive diseases of deterioration.

EXCESSIVE STRESS

When we speak of stress, we must actually differentiate between two different kinds of stress. There is "bad" stress, which can make our life miserable and make us sick. But there is also "good" stress, which motivates us, energizes us, and drives us to succeed and grow. Dealing appropriately with stress does not mean having no stress, for surely nothing could be more pointless or boring than never to be pushed or challenged, to sit on an idyllic hillside, smiling sweetly while the world goes by without us. Our bodies are made to handle stress: apparently, then, we are meant to grow, work, and succeed, to participate actively in all the challenges life presents. Problems arise only if we are truly overwhelmed with stress, or if we lose the ability to handle it. This becomes excessive or "bad" stress.

In the 1930s, the Nobel Prize winner Dr. Hans Selye began to publish his findings on stress.[1] His first insight was that many different factors cause stress: literally, stress is the wear-and-tear response of the body to any demand. This may include such factors as overwork, lack of sleep, emotional anxiety, extremes of heat or cold, diets high in sugar and coffee, or pain and illness themselves. But at the heart of Selye's brilliant research was the remarkable discovery that our body's response to stress is always the same. Under conditions of excessive stress, no matter what the cause, Selye found that three specific reactions always occur:

1. The *adrenal glands* begin to send out abnormal amounts of *hormones*
2. The spleen, thymus, and other related organs shrink in size, indicating *lowered immunity*
3. *Ulcers* begin to appear

The Adrenal Glands

The adrenal glands are among the body's endocrine glands, or organs that produce the chemical messengers we call hormones. These hormones provide the chemical control of our bodies' functions: they control the rate at which food is burned for energy; they control growth and repair; they coordinate blood sugar levels, sexual response, bone density, and so forth. Because these hormones are absorbed into the bloodstream, they sooner or later reach every cell in the body. We have discovered many important functions of these substances, but by no means do we understand everything they do. Indeed, we have not even found every hormone the body produces. What we do know is that tiny amounts of these substances can lead to dramatic changes, and they can do so in every single cell in our body. Some of these effects are immediate, others begin slowly; some are short-lived, others may persist for weeks or months. The endocrine system is both powerful and delicate. Among the most important adrenal hormones are aldosterone, cortisone, and adrenaline.

Aldosterone controls the amount of water and salt that the body retains or eliminates in the urine. This control helps to determine the *volume* of blood in the body, which thus helps determine the *pressure* of blood in the body. In other words, if excessive stress affects our adrenals, the altered production of aldosterone in turn may indirectly affect our blood pressure.

Cortisone has two important jobs: one, it helps to keep our blood sugar in balance, and two, it is anti-inflammatory. The body primarily uses sugar molecules (which are just tiny pieces of large carbohydrate molecules) to burn for energy. Any time our body needs energy, if the conveniently available sugar in the blood (from recently eaten food) is used up, it is the job of cortisone to convert stored fat and protein into sugar. Thus if our adrenals are not functioning as well as they should, we may have trouble maintaining appropriate blood sugar levels and consequently experience fatigue, irritability, and depression. Most of us respond to this fatigue by ingesting sweets, refined carbohydrates, and coffee. Although we can thereby temporarily replace blood sugar—and thus feel a "lift"—these stimulants are, in themselves, adrenal stressors. As we become increasingly dependent on candy and coffee, our adrenals become weaker, the fatigue intensifies, and the need for candy and coffee increases even more: a destructive cycle just keeps getting worse.

The other effect of cortisone is its anti-inflammatory action. Whenever any tissue is damaged, inflammation ensues. In this process, water, white blood cells, clotting elements, and other healing elements rush to the scene. Inflammation is part of an appropriate and necessary healing process. A problem may develop, however, if the process gets out of control—that is, if the inflammation (which is itself painful) persists when no longer needed, because the body's *anti*-inflammatory mechanisms (such as the production of adrenal cortisone) are not functioning up to par. You can see, for instance, how stress could thus turn a minor injury into a chronic swelling. This is why artificial cortisone shots are sometimes given after an injury, and why artificial cortisone pills such as Prednisone are often prescribed for patients with organic inflammations such as colitis (inflammation of the intestines). As always, pain is the body's way of announcing that there is a problem, but the problem is not a lack of Prednisone. Such symptoms indicate that the body's own anti-inflammatory mechanisms need help. Cortisone pills or shots, with their serious potential side-effects, can never maintain the qualitative or quantitative balance of a properly functioning, healthy endocrine system.

Adrenaline, the third adrenal hormone, mediates what we call the body's "fight or flight" mechanism. In a demanding situation, when adrenaline is released by the adrenal glands, the muscles receive extra blood, the cells receive extra sugar for energy, the eyes dilate, and the heart beats faster. If a wild animal is attacking us, we are ready, physiologically speaking, either to fight like crazy or to run like crazy. But in our usual, daily world, what do we do under pressure? When the boss fires us, it rarely helps to punch him in the nose. When the girlfriend leaves, we usually do not sprint away and climb the tallest tree. When the bills are overdue, the job is a bore, the kids are unmanageable, or the Russians aren't cooperating, what do we do with all that extra energy supplied by nature for "fight or flight"? Most of us turn it inside: we tighten our jaws, shoulders, and hips, squeeze our guts, grit our teeth, and go on with the day, deluding ourselves that we are just fine. Clearly, more appropriate ways to deal with this heightened energetic tension would be through physical exercise, creative work, intentional relaxation, or regular, honest expression of our needs, wishes, and feelings. But all too often if we have no outlet for pent-up fear, anger, or rage, we take it into the body. This inappropriate response is, of course, "bad" stress. Yet it becomes so habitual that most of us are not even aware that certain muscles have literally not relaxed for twenty years or more. Chronic tension means, in fact, that parts of our bodies are functionally dead. By deadening the body we deaden the mind and emotions as well, for the three are inseparable.

As stress continues to exhaust the adrenal glands, all our physiological functions suffer. Eventually, the body may have little or no ability left to resist. Symptoms subsequently no longer go away, and we end up, as Dr. Walter Schmitt notes, with "a variety of different complaints depending on which of the adrenals' functions have been the most compromised and the general areas of susceptibility which the patient has inherited or acquired."[2]

Adrenal exhaustion is not a "disease." It is a "condition" in which excessive stress has weakened our ability to *resist* disease. It is marked by many possible symptoms, any of which should alert you to take better care of yourself before things get worse:

- All the mentioned symptoms of low blood-sugar
- Excessive urination or perspiration
- Injuries that will not heal
- Joint aches and pains
- Anemia
- Any blood pressure problems
- Susceptibility to colds, flus, and infections
- Stomachaches
- Allergies
- Heart palpitations
- Headaches
- Asthma
- Hemorrhoids or varicose veins
- Cravings for sweets or caffeine
- Dizziness when standing up suddenly
- Maculinizing effects in females (such as growth of facial hair), or feminizing effects in males (such as increase in breast size)
- Muscle cramps or twitches
- Swelling
- Feeling "just plain sick"

Naturally, other factors besides adrenal exhaustion may also be involved in any of these symptoms. If you are concerned, see a professional.

Lowered Immunity

The second specific result of excessive stress that Selye documented, after adrenal exhaustion, is the lowering of our natural immunity. I have spoken already of how the body responds to any challenge or injury by initiating inflammation: the affected area is flooded with water, clotting elements, and masses of white blood cells. Thus armed, the body fights its invaders and repairs any damaged blood vessels.

Several factors are known to inhibit tissue repair—protein deficiency, an inadequate blood supply, and vitamin C deficiency, to name just a few. Yet although we know some of the ways in which we can interfere with the body's repair process, we do not know very much about how the body actually heals itself. We do know this: If you take a dead body and cut it, it will not heal. You can supply it with blood, white blood cells, histamine, water, protein, vitamin C, aspirin, alcohol, mercurochrome, and a Band-Aid, but it will not heal. Healing requires the innate intelligence of life.

Another factor in the immune response, in certain cases, is fever. When white blood cells attack a germ, they release a chemical into the blood that tells the brain to raise the body temperature. The reason for this is elegantly simple. There are millions of bacteria in the world, different types of which thrive in different temperatures. The only bacteria that can possibly hurt us are those that are capable of living in a climate of about 98.6 degrees. If those bacteria burn up and die in a temperature of 101 degrees, then it is a simple enough matter to raise the body temperature and kill them off. This is an example of nature's brilliant simplicity. Aspirin, which reduces the fever (a necessary defensive symptom) and thereby enhances the infection (an abnormal, potentially dangerous condition), is not nearly so brilliant. Aspirin makes you feel better if it does not upset your stomach, but it may keep you sicker longer. It is usually best to allow a mild fever to run its course. When your child's temperature is wildly out of control, of course you seek to control it. Even then, be aware that there seems to be a relationship between aspirin and Reye's Syndrome – a severe neurological and organic disease in children that is sudden in onset and often fatal. It is best to control a child's high temperature with lukewarm baths, or children's doses of alternative products like acetaminophen (Tylenol) if the baths do not work. But once the fever is under control, try to find out why things got out of control. And do not start dosing a child with Tylenol at the very first sign that the body is simply doing its job.

Selye and other researchers have found that under excessive stress, our immune structures (i.e., spleen, thymus, lymph nodes, tonsils) shrink. Most of our white blood cells are made by these structures; a hormone made by the thymus apparently activates them, and some white blood cells live their whole life within these structures, from whence they send out antibodies. What is most important, microscopic studies have confirmed that excessive or badly handled stress causes our white blood cells to decrease in both number and activity. As a result, our body's ability to defend us against disease is seriously compromised. If we now "catch" something, is it fair to say simply that the germ "caused" the problem? Is it reasonable to take a drug, and just leave it at that?

Ulcers

The third consistent result of excess stress is the formation of ulcers in the lining of the stomach. An ulcer is a kind of open sore. It is irritated by its constant contact with the highly acidic stomach juice, and moderate to severe pain can result, sometimes accompanied by nausea and vomiting. (Stomach acid in itself, incidentally, is not a bad thing; we need large quantities of acid to digest protein, we need it to digest calcium, and we need it to kill germs in the foods we eat.) If severe enough, an ulcer can even perforate the entire thickness of the stomach wall, causing a life-threatening situation.

The acid stomach juice causes an ulcer to hurt. But what caused the ulcer? The standard response is that somehow there was too much acid in the stomach, so that it burned a hole in the lining. But there is something very peculiar here. For one thing, it is known that under conditions of stress the stomach produces *less* acid. We also find that after the age of forty, the stomach tends to produce *less* acid. Yet the vast majority of ulcers occur in people over forty who are under enormous stress–the very people who are producing less acid!

Clearly, the theory of "too much" acid must be wrong. Ulcers appear when there is too little acid, not too much. Evidently, this lack of acidity causes abnormalities in digestion, and as a result the stomach lining becomes irritated and inflamed. If this inflammation persists, an ulcer will often result.

Once such an ulcer has appeared, it is necessary to create a soothing internal environment while it heals. Antacids may have temporary value, but they offer no more than that. Eating many small meals low in protein will keep down the concentration of acid. Comfrey and chlorophyll may be both soothing and healing. But let's talk about the prevention of ulcers, and the prevention of recurrences of ulcers. This means increasing the stomach's acidity. The old Vermont folk remedy of a spoonful of apple cider vinegar in some water at mealtimes is one approach. In fact, at the first sign of digestive trouble, before an ulcer appears, this is good advice. Another approach, particularly after age forty, is to cut down on the consumption of meat and other heavy proteins, because they require acid for digestion. Most people tend to do this on their own, sensing that they can no longer eat the big steak dinners they loved when they were twenty. Actually, though, these approaches mean either substituting for a task that a healthy body ought to do on its own, or avoiding the pleasure of a steak dinner. This is not how we ought to live. Part of being healthy means being able to do, in moderation, what we wish to do. If, for instance, your system has become so weakened by stress that you have developed multiple "food allergies," then "feeling better" by subsisting on a diet restricted to carrots does not mean you are healthy! Once your body has pushed you into a corner, becoming healthy requires figuring out what you have been doing wrong and correcting it patiently and lovingly. Do not settle for a lifetime of drugs or a lifetime of "avoidance." If you do, you are certain to encounter more symptoms and more things to avoid with each passing day.

So what can we do about ulcers?

Orthodox medicine says: Take Tagamet.

Holistic medicine says: Relax. Work on your emotions. Exercise and eat a healthy diet, including some healing herbs. If the overall aim of the individual is to grow and learn, then a symptom like an ulcer can be seen as a straightforward signal that something must be changed. If the overall aim is simply to remain as comfortable as possible, then the ulcer will only be seen as a great bother. This latter person will opt for the Tagamet, and the ulcer symptoms will, indeed, probably go away. He will be left, however, with the same level of stress, the same dietary problems, and the same psychological state. Nothing of lasting value has been accomplished, and the body may have to repeat its call for help by sending out a new symptom or by manifesting a recurrence of the old one. If he opts for the holistic route, the body may take a little longer to heal the ulcer, but once it does he will not be a sitting duck for a relapse or a new problem.

Our twentieth-century policy of laissez-faire leads us to allow the poisoning of the earth, the poisoning of our minds, and the poisoning of our bodies. Then, in order to remain comfortable, we invent increasingly stronger drugs to numb us from the painful, inevitable effects of these actions: ulcers, arteriosclerosis, arthritis, cancer. The premise is clearly unsound: an obvious point, but one that cannot be emphasized strongly enough. Yes, in life-or-death situations drugs are truly a blessing. For crisis intervention in emergencies they are truly a blessing. But the premise that drugs are the solution is unsound because the problem is viewed only in terms of the end results and the "solution" is to apply some sort of comfortable "Band-Aid" and falsely call it a cure. It is unsound because it ultimately has nothing to do with personal growth, optimal health, or a meaningful life. Nor is this merely a problem in the healing arts. As the incidence of chronic disease rises—and with it the demand for stronger medicinal drugs to numb our bodies—so also we see an ever-increasing demand for stronger recreational drugs to numb our minds. Indeed, the incidence of crime in our society follows the same path as the incidence of disease in the body. The processes go hand in hand.

POOR NUTRITION

Our modern diet constitutes the second major factor in the pervasive spread of cardiovascular disease, chronic inflammatory disease, and cancer. In chapter 4 I will discuss good nutrition fully; here I will just briefly discuss those harmful foods that should be reduced sharply in our diets. Let me note, too, that there is no need to become negative or to become a fanatic about "health food." This type of extreme attitude just becomes another unnecessary source of stress. Eating should never be a joyless burden. Eating should be a pleasure, a time to relax, a time to be with friends and loved ones, a time to enjoy the aesthetics of fine food and good company. The information available to us today regarding healthful and harmful dietary elements should enable us to make wise choices and to establish a balance for our own bodies.

We would do well to minimize the use of the following items:

Sugar

This category includes any foods that *contain* sugar, as well as artificial sweeteners. I have already discussed the added stress sugar puts on the adrenal glands, and it is well known that white blood cells become sluggish in the presence of sugar: too many sweets in the diet make us tired and fatigued, deficient in vitamins, and less resistant to illness. And of course, sugar rots our teeth and makes us fat.

Caffeine

Even decaffeinated coffee still retains some caffeine, and the usual decaffeination process may leave harmful chemical residues. Water-decaffeinated coffee, though far from being good for you, is probably the least harmful. Caffeine also creates nutritional stress, with ill effects on both the adrenal glands and the nervous system. Caffeine causes artificial peristalisis (the rhythmic contractions of the intestines). Over time, we can become addicted to coffee in such a way that we cannot have a normal bowel movement and must rely more and more on coffee to relieve constipation. Coffee consumption has also been implicated in the formation of breast cysts.

Refined Flours and Grains

Refined carbohydrates—white bread, white rice, and so on—are harmful in just the same ways that sugar is harmful. They also do not provide the important vitamins, minerals, and fiber that whole grains naturally supply, so that our cells are deprived of this source of steady, continuous energy. Finally—and this is very important—refined foods pass through our system so slowly that they have time to spoil, and possibly to cause the formation of carcinogens.

Alcohol

Alcohol is quickly converted in the body into simple sugar, and thus is another source of physiological stress. Alcoholism invariably brings nutritional disaster in its wake, along with all the other harmful effects. We need not deny alcohol's potential social and stress-relieving benefits but we do need to be careful.

Preservatives and Additives

Preservatives destroy natural enzymes, substances that are created by nature to help us digest our food. But since these same enzymes also contribute to eventual decomposition (which, after all, is the function of digestion), food companies add preservatives in order to increase their shelf life. Their presence lowers the food value; makes digestion, absorption, and utilization more difficult; and often has poisonous side effects. "Virtually every product on the market has been treated chemically at some time during its processing," author and journalist Gary Null has noted. He continues:

> Annually, one billion pounds of food additives are manufactured and processed into the food Americans eat, an average of nearly five pounds per person. The tools of the food technicians are endless: dyes, bleaches, emulsifiers, antioxidants, preservatives, flavorings, buffers, acidifiers, alkalizers, deodorants, moisteners, drying agents, extenders, thickeners, neutralizers, sweeteners, conditioners, disinfectants, maturers, fortifiers. These are just some of them. With these and other agents, the technician literally becomes a sorcerer who can beguile, deceive and defraud the consumer by making him think he's getting something he really isn't. This magic can make stale products seem fresh. It can substitute nutritionally valueless chemicals in place of natural foods. Almost without exception, these chemical instruments destroy vitamins, minerals and enzymes. As a result, the end food products

contain little, if any, of the life-supporting qualities of natural foods.[3]

To receive all the life-supporting properties of food, which nature intended to provide and which our bodies must have, we must eat fresh, untreated food.

Table Salt

Sodium is an extremely important nutrient, perhaps the most important element in the body. All of our cells are bathed in a sodium solution and cannot survive without it. But nature supplies it so abundantly that our use of added table salt becomes excessive and dangerous, particularly to the heart.

Pasteurization

This is the process of extreme heating to destroy all germs and enzymes. Unfortunately, the process affects all the useful bacteria and enzymes as well as the bad ones. For instance, pasteurization makes milk extremely difficult to digest and likely to irritate the intestinal walls.

Nicotine

Nicotine is a nervous-system narcotic. The Surgeon General of the United States has stated that cigarettes are involved in a wide variety of cancers and other serious illnesses. According to insurance company studies, smoking is the second most important variable, after genetic inheritance, in determining a person's life expectancy. One thousand Americans die each day from illnesses traceable to smoking. This is more than the total number killed by crack, alcohol, car accidents, AIDS, heroin, and murder combined.

Hydrogenated and Partially Hydrogenated Oils

These substances rank among the most harmful ones we ingest. As common as they are, they require some explanation.

The body has three basic mechanisms for combating inflammation: an adrenal hormone, *cortisone* (which I have discussed on page 15; *dietary anti-oxidants* (which I discuss on page 29) and a family of chemicals called *prostaglandins.*[4]

There are several varieties of prostaglandins, which together serve a number of functions. Broadly speaking, we can say that they fall into two general categories: proinflammatory, proclotting prostaglandins; and anti-inflammatory, anticlotting prostaglandins.

As we have seen, in order to heal damaged tissues and blood vessels following injury, we need the ability to generate inflammation and to clot blood. In addition, we need to be able to *control* inflammation and clotting. That is why the body, always striving for balance, makes both categories of prostaglandins. Ideally, our cells should be able to make enough of either, whenever needed. But unfortunately this is often no longer possible: our bodies tend to make many more "pro's" than "anti's." And the reason for this unhealthy imbalance is strictly a matter of diet.

To begin with, all the controlling "anti's" are made out of healthy vegetable oils and some cold-water fish oils. On the other hand, all the "pro's" are made from animal and dairy fats. So right from the start we see that a diet heavy in meat and dairy products, but low in fresh vegetables and oils, will tend to load us up with too many *pro*inflammatory, *pro*clotting, prostaglandins.

Second, several B vitamins assist in the production of the "anti's," while helping to slow down excessive production of "pro's." But on a diet of refined foods and few whole foods, we again encourage only the "pro's" because our food is deficient in vitamin B.

Third, we come to the hydrogenated, or partially hydrogenated, oils. These are originally healthy oils that food manufacturers have altered to prevent spoilage. Needless to say, this is a big advantage for the food industry. These products look like oil, taste like oil, smell like oil, and can be used in cooking just like oil—and they never spoil! But *food spoils.* Only plastic does not spoil. The breakdown of food when it spoils is actually rather similar to the breakdown of food when it is digested. The price we pay for making food unspoilable is its indigestibility. Such nonfood becomes useless at best, dangerous at worst. And hydrogenated oils are dangerous: they clog up the body's chemistry for turning healthy oils into anti-inflammatory, anticlotting, prostaglandins, and effectively stop their production.

When you put all three of the above factors together, you can see why our bodies must be producing many more of the "pro's," especially since supermarket labels reveal that the hydrogenated oils are nearly all-pervasive. They are used in breads, cakes, cookies, and other baked goods to ensure indefinite shelf-life. And because they are creamy (like margarine), they are a major ingredient in commercial peanut butter, mayonnaise, and other items that tempt us by promising to be creamier than the competition. They are also used in potato chips, peanuts, and all the greasy junk food.

What does this mean to you and me? It means that our bodies have an acquired tendency toward the formation of inflammation and blood clots that is virtually overwhelming – and barely any power left to control it. It means that arthritis and colitis and heart attacks and strokes have to be on the rise! Furthermore, recent reports in the medical literature indicate that the anticlotting, anti-inflammatory prostaglandins are *antiviral* as well. They thus may have an impact on virus-dependent cancers, on AIDS, on colds and flus, and on infectious diseases in general. This is not to say that a diet of partially hydrogenated oils "causes" viral illness or inflammation, or anything so simplistic. I am speaking here of just one factor of causality: the body's receptivity. A poor diet can create unhealthy internal conditions, as a result of which a relatively weak active agent may then become capable of initiating a disease that a properly balanced body would never have permitted. Because of the vast importance of the prostaglandin system, it is advisable to supplement the diet with rich sources of the appropriate oils, particularly the essential fatty acids called GLA and EPA.

Not long ago, we had no idea how aspirin, ibuprofen (Motrin), steroids, and the other anti-inflammatory drugs worked. Now we know that these various drugs *stop the production of all pros-*

taglandins. As a result, instead of having an *imbalance* of prostaglandins, we end up with virtually none at all! Of course this
will help relieve symptoms: We are so overloaded with "pro's"
that it could hardly do otherwise.

But surely it would be wiser to use a healthy diet to lower the
excessive amount of "pro's" and to return the "anti's" back to their
appropriate levels. Such a process would be healing the body,
rather than interfering with the body.

Instead, some doctors suggest that we deal with this situation
by taking an aspirin a day. Heart attacks are not caused by a
deficiency in aspirin! To avoid a tendency to form blood clots to
the heart, we need to exercise properly, relax, and eat a healthy
diet. We cannot continue to do everything wrong and then
expect anti-inflammatory drugs to be the magic cure. The latter
belief explains why Motrin and all its generic equivalents are
now sold over the counter. Our bodies are so burdened with
hydrogenated oils that millions of people are now dependent
upon this drug. We are being sold poison one day, and a drug to
appease our symptoms the next day. Rather than fight the body
with a daily drug, we can heal the body by taking care of
ourselves naturally.

ENVIRONMENTAL POLLUTION

After stress and poor nutrition, pollution provides the third major
factor in the three particular types of illness our society faces.
Millions of Americans live in areas where the air does not meet even
the minimum air quality standards of the federal government. Lead
from industrial and automobile emissions can lead to learning
disabilities and various other serious health problems. Emissions
from diesel engines cause cancer and respiratory disease. Gar-
bage incinerators dump toxins into the air, including dioxin,
perhaps the most lethal chemical mankind has developed. Sulfur
and nitrogen emissions from smokestacks cause respiratory illnesses. Chlorofluorocarbons have damaged the atmosphere's
protective ozone layer, leading to cancer and eye problems.[5]

Our water is routinely filled with lead, mercury, pesticides,
industrial sludge, human and animal waste, and other toxic and

carcinogenic chemicals. In recent years, underground injection of hazardous waste has become a major means of disposal, even though it poisons groundwater, a major source of drinking water.

Virtually all Americans (over 99 percent) have detectable amounts of pesticides, fungicides, and insecticides in their bodies. These chemicals have been found to cause cancer, birth defects, nervous system problems, and genetic mutations. Drugs such as penicillin and tetracycline are fed daily to farm animals, and these cause germs to mutate and become resistant. These drugs, which show up in the meat we eat, are not fed to animals simply to keep them healthy: when taken in large quantities, they artificially produce rapid growth. How and why this happens is unknown.

Most recently, the food industry has gotten together with the nuclear energy people and the FDA to offer us something new. They now wish to preserve our food by exposing it to extremely high levels of radiation. The FDA acknowledges that it does not know what effect such radiation might have on the nutrient quality of food. The agency has also acknowledged that it does not even have the technology to test for safety! But by killing germs and bugs, radiation does preserve food, so claims are made that it will help feed the hungry and eliminate the need for chemicals. (Since the bugs and germs are not permanently eradicated by treating any particular food with radiation, however, there is actually no intention at all of eliminating the use of chemicals).

Recent studies indicate that the world's food supply is more than ample—only financial greed and politics are keeping our fellow human beings hungry. The real reason the collaborating industries want to irradiate our food is simple: food irradiation plants use the waste from nuclear reactors, thereby substantially reducing the disposal cost of nuclear waste. Thus the United States government has sanctioned dangerous technology, permitting us to tamper with processes we do not understand, making a great deal of money for some few at the risk of the health, indeed the lives, of millions of human beings.

An interesting aspect of the action of our white blood cells is their production of chemicals called "free radicals." These free radicals are portions of large molecules that have become separated from the original molecule. A free radical has a wildly energized area of intense electrical negativity; natural forces drive this free radical to connect with something positive and thus to become stabilized. During its frenzied search for a positive particle, the free radical is bursting with explosive force. And since it sometimes only stabilizes by stealing the positive portion of another molecule (and thereby releasing that molecule's negative half as a new free radical), one free radical can initiate a vicious cycle in which more and more wild free radicals are perpetually being generated.

Why would our white blood cells produce these things? When the white blood cell sees an invader that it wants to devour, it first sends out a volley of free radicals to shoot it full of holes; only then does it approach the bacteria, or toxic chemical, or cancer cell.

Useful though they may be, however, it is crucial that these "chemical bullets" be quickly neutralized: otherwise, after they have done their job, they will go on to damage healthy tissue, causing irritation, inflammation, and premature aging. If not neutralized completely, they may begin a vicious cycle of tissue destruction that in turn may lead to a vicious cycle of inflammation. (This is the process in progressive arthritis, colitis, multiple sclerosis, and most other chronic inflammatory diseases.)

To prevent this, the body normally has a perfect mechanism to neutralize free radicals before they begin tearing into healthy tissue. As soon as they have done their job for the white blood cell, they are "quenched" by anti-oxidants. The various anti-oxidants (parallel to the various types of free radicals) include portions of vitamins A, C, and E, plus selenium, a liver enzyme called S.O.D., and a special trio of amino acids called glutathione. In addition, in order for the anti-oxidants to work properly, they need a number of cofactors such as B-6, zinc, and niacin.

So one can see how a bad diet could lead to a problem with anti-oxidants. So, too, could an overwhelming abundance of free radicals. And it turns out that vast numbers of free radicals are generated by

- *Radiation* (including fallout, X-rays, and the various dangerous rays that reach us now that we have damaged the earth's protective ozone layer)
- *Metal Poisoning* (including lead, mercury, copper, etc.)
- *Air Pollution* (including CO_2, cigarette smoke, gasoline fumes, industrial smog, etc.)

Our polluted environment is placing an enormous load on the body's anti-oxidant system, making tissue damage, premature aging, and chronic inflammation inevitable. Ideally, nutritional supplements should only be necessary occasionally and temporarily, until the body is restored to balance and we are eating healthy food. But with the destruction of the earth's environment we have destroyed the "ideal"; it may be necessary to supplement our diets with anti-oxidants forever.

Thus we see that there are abundant poisons and germs that can easily begin to act on our unbalanced bodies, once stress and malnutrition have rendered them receptive to disease. We can also see that our highly pressured lives, and our destructive and self-destructive attitudes, are all that is needed to maintain and intensify our difficulties. And we shall specifically see that the inevitable result of this is an increasing pervasiveness of cardio-vascular disease, chronic inflammatory disease, and cancer.

CARDIOVASCULAR DISEASE

The heart is the center of the human being. It impels the blood to every cell and fiber. The blood is diffused through the lungs to pick up oxygen, is passed along the intestines to assimilate food and water, and is filtered through the liver and kidneys to be cleansed. It brings warmth and nourishment to every corner of the body. This is all accomplished by the power of the heart.

Blood that enters the heart has little oxygen left and is filled with carbon dioxide waste. The heart pumps this blood to the lungs, where CO_2 is taken away and fresh oxygen is taken in.

This aerated blood then returns immediately to the heart, which now pumps it out to the rest of the body via the arteries. Immediately at this juncture, coronary arteries double back to supply the heart itself with nutritious, oxygen-rich blood. If the blood is not being pumped properly, or if a coronary artery is blocked by cholesterol plaques or clots, the heart will not receive its own needed blood supply, and it will ultimately stop. It must be fed, too.

Blood pressure is the pressure the blood exerts in an outward direction against the artery walls. Imagine the increase in pressure within an artery, if the amount of blood stays the same but its available passageway gets narrower and narrower, due to thick accumulations of cholesterol coating the inner vessel walls. Hypertension (which has nothing to do with nervous tension but merely means high blood pressure) causes the heart to work so hard to push the blood through such narrow passages that—like any overexercised muscle—the heart can grow in size. Unfortunately, this bulky growth is not accompanied by any increase in nutritious blood available in the coronary arteries. As a result, the now oversized muscle cannot get enough food and oxygen to sustain itself. Its "hunger pangs" cause painful muscle spasms, a condition called "angina pectoris." Nitroglycerine will relieve these spasms, and can often be life-saving. This sort of intervention at a crucial moment with a powerful drug is an example of medicine at its best.

When a blood vessel is injured, sticky particles called platelets rush to the cut or injured surface. If a cut or rupture is large, the platelets signal the "clotting reaction," so that a blood clot is formed to help stop up the wound. Over thirty different chemicals have been found to be required for clotting. Among the most important are vitamin K, calcium, and the prostaglandins. An *abnormal* clot (one serving no purpose) may also be formed, as a result of irritation to a blood vessel wall. Typical irritation would be caused by high blood pressure pressing against the rough surface of a cholesterol plaque (the rough surface mimics an injured surface and thus mistakenly brings on the clotting reaction). If such a clot breaks loose, and begins to be carried along in the blood flow, it may get stuck in a small, narrow vessel. If this happens, cells and tissue beyond that point will lose their blood supply due to the blockage, and hence will die of starvation. If a tiny clot blocks a tiny capillary and a few cells die, other cells will replace them and the problem is insignificant. But if a big clot blocks an artery to the brain, the resulting destruction of brain cells is called a stroke. If it blocks a coronary artery, thus killing part of the heart, it is called a heart attack. Phlebitis is the name for a similar process in a limb.

Atherosclerosis is a condition in which potential clot-causing plaques are deposited all along the inner arterial walls. These always contain cholesterol and may sometimes also contain the mineral calcium, in which case the arteries become extremely hard. This is then called arteriosclerosis, or simply "hardening of the arteries." Almost half of all people die of arteriosclerosis!

When any of these conditions occur—high blood pressure, angina pectoris, stroke, heart attack, phlebitis, atherosclerosis, or arteriosclerosis—we look to medicine for a cure. But there is no cure; there are only palliative measures or preventive measures. The former belong to the realm of medicine, the latter to what we are interested in here: Why is cardiovascular disease so prevalent in the United States?

Stress

Stress uses up B vitamins, which—as we will see in chapter 4— are necessary for proper cholesterol utilization. Adrenaline has various effects on blood *flow;* aldosterone is an important determinant of blood *pressure.* The balanced production of these adrenal hormones is adversely affected by stress. And, of course, emotional stress and anxiety can sometimes cause the heart to lose its steady electrical rhythm.

Diet

Refined diets leave us deficient in vitamin B. Add the factor of a diet high in animal fats and hydrogenated oils and low in fresh vegetable oils, and two consequences must follow: first, the body becomes unable to use cholesterol properly, and second, huge imbalances occur in prostaglandins, with greatly disproportionate numbers of the proclotting types appearing. Refined diets also disturb the intestinal flora, thus lowering our vitamin K levels and upsetting the clotting mechanism. Sugar and coffee cause all the problems of stress, while salt consumption raises blood pressure by inducing the body to retain water.

Pollution

Along with the massive stress caused by our polluted environment, many specific dangers to cardiovascular health have been isolated. For instance, cigarette smoke has been found to have a definite link to heart disease. And free radicals have been found to irritate the coronary arteries, thus initiating deadly clots. Mercury has been associated with heart problems, as have many other environmental pollutants.

High blood pressure, cholesterol plaques, and abnormal bloodclots are all directly linked to stress, poor nutrition, and pollution. Seen in this light, the contemporary prevalence of cardiovascular disease is no mystery.

CHRONIC INFLAMMATORY DISEASE

Some degree of inflammation occurs in almost every type of illness. The symptoms we feel will vary, depending on where the inflammation is—but the inflammation itself, wherever it is, is always remarkably similar. The inflammation-response is the most common and most important of the changes the body undergoes as a result of disease. It is also painful and annoying, and if it persists it can be destructive, which is why our bodies are protected with three anti-inflammatory mechanisms.

Arthritis is a much-misunderstood word that simply means "inflammation of a joint." In other words, any time a joint is inflamed for any reason, it is an arthritis. It may be mild or severe, it may last an hour or a lifetime, it may be caused by an injury or a virus. Arthritis, then, is not "a" particular disease. There are at least fifty known types of arthritis.

Rheumatoid arthritis involves inflammation of a synovial capsule (a structure within certain joints that behaves much like a lubricating ball bearing). As a result of this inflammation, hard fibrous tissue may form to replace adjacent soft, malleable tissue, causing pain, loss of mobility, and visible deformities. Calcium deposits form in the joint. Although all these reactions represent the body's attempt to halt any further deterioration, they are in themselves extremely painful and destructive.

Gout, or gouty arthritis, is a metabolic problem involving a chemical called purine. A waste product of improper purine metabolism ends up being deposited inside a joint, and this causes irritation and chronic inflammation.

Osteoarthritis is due to wear and tear in joints, usually the vertebral joints of the spine. Perhaps caused by chronic malalignment (brought on by the millions of minor bumps and bruises we receive in our lives), the resultant excessive and improper rubbing between joint surfaces causes irritation and inflammation. The surfaces of bones are rich with pain-sensing nerve endings, which is why this disease hurts so much.

You can see from just these few examples that the idea of "a" cure for arthritis is impossible. Even if some magic pill could correct purine metabolism, how could it also affect synovial capsules and bone surfaces? The inflammation is the same, but the problems are different. The drugs we use for arthritis (such as aspirin and ibuprofen) are used to combat inflammation generally, by eliminating all our prostaglandins. But this is certainly not a cure.

Gastritis is inflammation of the stomach. Appendicitis is inflammation of the appendix. Colitis in inflammation of the colon. Bronchitis, cystitis, meningitis, dermatitis . . . the list goes on and on. Degenerative inflammatory diseases are rampant in America today. They vary because of various inherited or acquired susceptibilities, and because of various secondary factors. But they are all similar, and they are all interrelated. Let's review why:

Stress

When the body is exhausted by stress, among the many significant problems created is the drop in production of the anti-inflammatory hormone cortisone. In addition, the whole functioning of the immune system is lowered.

Diet

Diets of animal fats, refined carbohydrates, and partially hydrogenated oils present us with a continual huge overdose of pro-inflammatory prostaglandins (and hardly any compensating anti-inflammatory prostaglandins).

Pollution

Toxic metals, chemicals, toxic gases, and radiation are among the poisons that create masses of inflammation-inducing free radicals, and our dietary intake of the "quenching" anti-oxidants cannot keep up with the demand.

We have been deluded into believing such notions as "A little arthritis is normal as you get older." Therefore we obediently support the industries that poison our food and environment, just as we obediently support the industries that daily foist new "miracle" drugs upon us. And the inflammatory diseases have become more and more pervasive.

CANCER

One of the most inexplicable of life's surprises is the process called *cell differentiation*. The human child begins as one cell, which divides into two identical cells, then four identical cells, then eight, sixteen, and so on into the trillions. Along the way, some of these identical cells miraculously begin to turn into nerve cells, while others become bone cells, and still others become red blood cells. How do they know? How does one cell in the sixteenth generation of daughter cells know to begin differentiating into a brain cell, while the one next to it begins differentiating into something else? Originally, they were all exact duplicates of the one cell!

Another miracle occurs when healthy bodily tissue is damaged and the nearby remaining healthy cells make duplicates of themselves in order to replace their fallen brethren. Who told them to do this? And when all the tissue has been repaired, and the duplication stops, who tells them it is time to stop? We can describe this healing process in nearly all its elegant detail, but we cannot explain it. We do not understand the miracle of normal cellular growth.

It is little wonder, then, that we do not understand abnormal cellular growth. How is it that sometimes a cell turns all its energies into the mindless process of endless reproduction? Why, at the expense of all useful functioning (such as hormone synthesis, nerve transmission, bone reconstruction, bacteria fighting, enzyme production, and all the thousands of useful functions our cells normally perform), would a cell suddenly become totally useless—and yet absorb massive quantities of nutrients in order to wildly reproduce millions of its own useless kind? Why would one crazy cell (or several) begin a cancerous chain reaction that can kill an entire being by sapping its energy and blocking its functions?

Or perhaps there is an even more important question than "Why does cancer happen?" Why does the rest of the body permit it?

A normal cell is able to produce energy with or without oxygen, but the job is much more difficult and inefficient without it. A cancer cell has no choice but to go without oxygen, so that these cells are forced to steal all the body's nutrients in order to keep up with their ever-growing energy demand. As a result, the cancer victim wastes away. But why does the body allow these cancer cells such preferential treatment? Why don't the healthy cells demand this food and energy, and let the cancer cells starve? Why does the body allow them to get away with this?

Our genetic structure is unfathomably intricate and delicate. The system can thus be interfered with in many ways, any of which can cause mutations in genes. So it must be understood that there is no single cause of cancer. Cancer, like inflammation, is not so much a disease as a process – in this case, one that has gone lethally wrong. And again three factors can be seen to be involved:

1. Various factors may *initiate* this process. We call these factors "carcinogens" (the *active cause*).
2. Various factors help to *maintain* this process. We call these "co-carcinogens" (the *receptive cause*).
3. Finally, the body's immune system must *allow* this process (the *conciliatory cause*).

Cancer is not merely an attack by an outside agent. Cancer is something our own cells do.

In today's polluted environment it is easy for an occasional cancerous mutation to occur. But such a mutated cell is abnormal, and the function of the immune system is to get rid of anything that is abnormal. It is therefore believed that our bodies regularly produce a few random cancer cells. We only "get cancer" if our immune system fails to deal with them. And it will only fail to do so if something is already wrong; if the immune system is functioning perfectly, no problem will arise.

Only sick people get cancer. Such a statement, on first glance, may sound silly or redundant. But think about it for a moment. One's natural defenses against disease must already be lowered – in other words, one must already be sick – in order for a cancer to take hold and spread. And we are all sick to some degree: in this world of high stress, malnutrition, and pollution, none of us can claim that everything is working perfectly.

Of course one's defenses can simply be overwhelmed, such as will no doubt happen to many of the unfortunate human beings who lived in or near Chernobyl and Three Mile Island at the time of those nuclear accidents. But such extreme scenarios, so far, are still rare. For a healthy immune system, doing battle with a few occasional cancer cells should be a routine matter. In the field of orthodox medicine, cancer researchers almost exclusively continue to look for the single pill or treatment that will "cure" cancer. For the blessings of pain relief and help for the victims among us, of course this crucial research must go on. But there is also the important question of why our immune systems allow such a problem to begin with, what multiplicity of factors interfere with normal immune response, and how we can eliminate these interferences. Because the cancer is not the real sickness. The cancer is the *result* of the sickness. The cancer is the symptom. Symptoms are what tell us that something is wrong. They tell us when it is time to change.

Cancer. One of the most frightening of all words. Why has it become so common? Again, there are three factors at work:

Stress

Stress weakens the entire immune system. The thymus and other lymph tissue shrink, while white blood cells diminish in both numbers and effectiveness. The body, remember, does not distinguish among different types of stressors. Too much uncoped-with stress of any type, physical or psychological, will weaken the ability of the immune system to fight invaders, including germs, carcinogenic chemicals, and intermitten cancer cells themselves.

Diet

Refined carbohydrates, sugar, alcohol, and deficiencies in vitamin C have all been shown to make white blood cells sluggish. Refined carbohydrates, animal fats, and well-done meats are known to travel so slowly through out intestines that they spoil — a process that has been clearly linked to cancer. Diets low in fresh vegetables leave us deficient in cancer-preventing fiber and low in cancer-fighting anti-oxidants.

Pollution

Radiation, smoke, and all the countless carcinogens in our food, water, and air threaten us continually.

The prevalence of cancer is not a mystery; it is not a coincidence; it has nothing to do with bad luck. We are given poison, and we accept it. We are given drugs to appease the symptoms, and we are grateful. We are told the most blatant of lies, and we quietly go along with them. It is a prescription for death.

But as we shall see, we do not need to keep filling this prescription. Studies invariably show that the great majority of people who overcome these illnesses are the ones who take control of their lives, change their habits and situations, and decide to put up a good fight. And even if they do not always succeed completely, at least the time spent in living is more meaningful and joyful than the time wasted in dying.

2

Confronting the
AIDS Epidemic

And now, in addition to these typical contemporary diseases, a terrible new syndrome, recalling some ancient plague, has appeared to shake up our complacency and to challenge our intellect, our emotions, and our will.

More than 60,000 of our fellow human beings – men, women, and children – have already died of AIDS. It is believed that more than a million of us have been exposed to the HIV virus that is said to cause it. Over the next few years, according to a conservative estimate, hundreds of thousands of deaths will occur. The figures are so staggering as to be incomprehensible, abstract, and finally numbing. Still, as Albert Camus noted in his celebrated novel *The Plague,* "When abstraction sets to killing you, you've got to get busy with it."

In 1983, Dr. Robert Gallo of the National Institutes of Health announced the discovery of a viral cause of AIDS. Unlike bacterial infections, which occur *among* our cells, viruses cause problems *inside* our cells where they usurp the cells' genetic structure in order to force the creation of more viruses like themselves. Hence they are extremely difficult to tackle. Antibiotic drugs, for instance, cannot reach viruses inside our cells and thus have no effect on them (which is why it is a waste of time and money, and only risks side effects, to take penicillin for a cold or flu). In fact, this brings up one of the real dreads about viral illness: medical science has never yet found a substance that can enter our cells and effectively kill active viruses without also harming us. Infectious viral diseases have been stopped in several ways. Most, like the common cold, are self-limiting. For some we have invented vaccines, which, by artificially stimulating the body to produce extra quantities of its own protective counteragents before there is an infection, effectively prevent healthy people from later catching the disease. In the case of airborne, easily transmitted diseases like smallpox (but totally unlike AIDS), we can quarantine the patient to protect others, and wait for the disease to run its course. But in none of these examples is a medical means available to cure a patient who has already contracted the viral illness.

We know that (with the rarest possible exceptions) AIDS is clearly not self-limiting. And quarantining patients would achieve nothing of any conceivable value. Medical research in AIDS has therefore focused on several goals: (1) a safe, effective vaccine; (2) better means of treating the secondary opportunistic infections, most importantly Kaposi's sarcoma (KS) and pneumocystis pneumonia (PCP); (3) stronger means whereby to bolster the damaged immune system; (4) the invention of a virus-killing but life-preserving drug: this last presents an awesome scientific challenge. Research goes on against the clock, yet it is a sad commentary that the Pentagon's expenditures every few days are higher than the total federal expenditure for AIDS during the entire epidemic.

AIDS is supposedly caused by the cruelly destructive yet fragile HIV virus, which dies instantly when it is removed from the environment of warm body fluids. It is a difficult disease to contract when looked at from the point of view of a laboratory microscope. But from the point of view of human relationships, and habits, it appears a relatively easy disease to contract. It would only waste precious time to be terror-stricken or morally self-righteous, but we likewise cannot afford to be uninterested or unconcerned. None of these are sufficient feelings with which to confront a plague! The human race has contracted AIDS. In addition to supporting research, following preventive measures, and finding better ways to educate ourselves and our children in a positive, sensible, and respectful approach to sexuality, several issues cry out to be pondered.

Where did this HIV virus come from? Has it existed in a dormant state, for thousands of years? Did it suddenly appear out of "nowhere"? Did it recently evolve from a less dangerous germ purely by chance? Perhaps one of these possibilities is the case. But we would be wise to consider, as a spur to future wisdom and caution, that such a germ may have evolved as a consequence of human activities. It may have existed in a harmless form since time immemorial, until our polluting, destructive manipulation of the environment somehow forced it to mutate into something deadly, or simply rendered our unfortunate bodies more receptive to it. The most awful possibility, of course—and one for which there is a disturbing amount of evidence—is that it came out of research into germ warfare and somehow got loose.[1] Even if this is so, establishing definite proof may not be possible at this point. But it is crucial for us to remember that research into chemical and biological warfare can only increase the probability that such an event may one day take place—be it accidentally, stupidly, or maliciously. If we keep this up, either overtly or covertly, something grotesque is going to happen. A third possibility is that abuse of medical drugs has led, via the tendency of germs to evolve into drug-resistant strains, to a series of direct and indirect microbial mutations, culminating with the HIV virus, or perhaps several such germs. For a long time we have been overutilizing drugs—prescribing them indiscriminately for every minor infection or illness, feeding them to our cattle and poultry, and selling them greedily over the counter in Third World countries. As a result of this abuse, we are confronted today with ever more resistant germs. Sooner or later, one of these resistant, mutant microbes, which we ourselves have brought into existence by our continual interference with nature, is going to get *us* before we get *it*. Hopefully, this scenario is not the case with AIDS. But what about the next germ? As long as we continue this behavior, there will inevitably be a next germ. All the wrong thoughts and all the wrong attitudes we have about health and disease, science and nature, have brought us to this deadly impasse. For we continue to think that we are smarter than nature, and that rather than having any obligation to her, all we have is the right and duty to dominate her. Eventually this thoughtless abuse is going to unleash a perilous new microbe. Or perhaps it has already happened.

The major issue demanding our common consideration is the question of how we are now going to treat each other. In times of previous plagues, families and friends often fled from each other in times of need, due to the fear of contagion. In the case of AIDS, we know the disease cannot be spread through simple proximity or casual contact. In previous plagues, fear aroused a need for scapegoats: during the Black Death of the fourteenth century, thousands of Jews were burned alive, despite the pope's plea to recognize that Jews were suffering from the plague in the same proportions as everyone else. Rather than looking for modern scapegoats, each of us individually can use our minds for prevention and education, and we can use our hearts for compassion and for the care of those among us who suffer.

But there is a great deal more to this story, and a great many questions that must be asked about this peculiar new virus that is being accused of causing such a wide spectrum of diverse physical symptoms around the world.

Dr. Peter Duesberg, a molecular biologist with the University of California, in 1987 concluded research at the National Institutes of Health in Maryland. He has long been a key participant in both cancer and AIDS research, working closely with Robert Gallo and other top scientists at NIH. Duesberg is one of several experts who have asserted unequivocally that HIV has not been shown to be the cause of AIDS.[2]

There are certain accepted scientific criteria for ascertaining whether or not a particular germ causes a particular disease. The HIV theory has never been proven by these rigorous standards. First of all, the virus cannot be found in every diagnosed case of AIDS; indeed, some studies have been able to find it in as few as 50 percent of patients. Second, when HIV is inoculated into lab animals, AIDS does not result. This has always been a necessary step before claiming that a germ causes an illness. Moreover, of the many cases of accidental inoculation into *human* researchers, only a fraction have gone on to develop AIDS. Third, while pathogenic organisms are known to produce poisonous substances – or at least to be rampantly replicating during active illnesses – the HIV virus appears to be virtually dormant, doing nothing at all, throughout the course of AIDS. It shows no biological activity that would account for any sickness. Finally, if AIDS were simply the result of a highly contagious virus, then by now the disease would certainly have exploded (as predicted in the early 1980s) into the American heterosexual community—yet it hasn't. In short, a careful examination of scientific literature fails to produce any conclusive evidence that HIV causes AIDS. Such proof may yet be found, or—more likely—it may be found that HIV plays some part in the problem. But all that can be stated with certainty so far is that HIV is noticeably present in communities where AIDS exists. But so are many other factors. "Many AIDS patients have the herpes virus too," notes Duesberg, "but no one is saying that herpes causes AIDS."

Since the virus cannot be found in many AIDS patients, what exactly defines an accurate diagnosis of the disease? What *is* AIDS? According to the official definition from the Centers for Disease Control (CDC) in Atlanta, the AIDS syndrome can include any of a variety of symptoms, any number of which can be considered conclusively diagnostic and all of which result from a badly damaged immune system: bacterial infections, cancers, fungal and yeast infections, viral infections, skin disorders—the detailed list actually goes on for many pages. "The various definitions of AIDS, used to make diagnoses around the world, are useless and vague," writes Jon Rappaport in *AIDS Inc.* "They allow almost anyone to be pinned with the label, AIDS."

Actually, there are no scientific grounds for saying that AIDS is any one thing. And it is scientifically unheard-of to claim that a single virus causes one set of symptoms among Africans, an essentially different set of symptoms among IV drug users, and yet another set of symptoms among male homosexuals. Most important of all, the entire list of AIDS symptoms have been with us for a long time and can be attributed to many other causes. The most common and potent cause of severe immunosuppression is hunger and malnutrition. The two most significant AIDS-related illnesses, KS and PCP, have long been known to exist among the hungry of the earth. PCP epidemics were reported in Europe during World War II and again in Vietnam in the 1970s.

Many prescriptive drugs are strongly immunosuppressive. KS has been reported in this country as a reaction to excessive treatment with the anti-inflammatory drug Prednisone. In fact, all of the so-called symptoms of AIDS can be easily brought about by drug abuse, whether from recreational drugs or excessive antibiotics and other medicinal drugs.

Stress, whether physical or emotional, weakens the immune system. Poisonous environmental chemicals weaken the immune system. Radiation weakens the immune system. Add to this a long history of recurrent sexually transmitted disease or concurrent, continuous drug abuse, and one can see why severe immunosuppression is prevalent among many homosexuals and IV drug users. Or add the powerful factor of hunger, and one sees why it is also prevalent in many Third World countries. All the best evidence indicates that the HIV virus is just one more opportunistic infection, and perhaps not even a very important one.

AIDS is not "one" disease, and it is not caused by "one" factor. It is a multifaceted *syndrome* brought about by *many* factors. Why, then, are we daily being terrorized by the formula HIV = AIDS = DEATH? According to Laurence Badgely, M.D., "The multifactorial model is a threat to the well-being of the international pharmaceutical giants, megalithic national research institutions, and aspirant Nobel Laureates. Most devastatingly, this model does not extrapolate to a single magic-bullet cure."[3]

The AIDS epidemic, with all the horror it has brought upon humanity, is not to be belittled. But for that very reason we must be wary not to use the grimness of the situation as an excuse for refusing to question official explanations. Because if the official explanation is wrong, it is hindering prevention and allowing people to die. That would make it not just wrong, but vicious.

People are not being decently fed. People are subtly being encouraged to lead unsafe, unhealthy life-styles. People are living and working in poisoned environments. If, however, we blame any resulting ills on the "AIDS virus," no one must feel guilty about promoting policies and attitudes that lead to hunger, poverty, or pollution. The face-saving smokescreen provided by this new germ is very convenient.

There are social factors . . . in the whole presumption that every disease has a single agent. Some people want to believe that nothing we do in our lives, in our environments, is really unhealthy. That poverty is really not a bad thing, just a choice, and it doesn't make people sick. That sexual behaviour and lifestyles are really harmless. The single-agent idea of disease, when believed across the board, at the expense of environmental factors, absolves people whose economic policies create ghettos and keep people poor. It's so easy to say that a virus came along and made people sick, not their living conditions. People who live a highly promiscuous lifestyle prefer to believe that the really lethal effects are external to that life, and are from a virus that comes along. Or in Africa, it's much easier to say that illness from the collapse of malaria-eradication programs or hunger, is really due to HIV.

We're hung up on high-tech solutions. The one-agent theory is going to be attractive to researchers. All the funding went that way. It's also the attraction of the quick-fix, the quick cure.[4]

In the 1950s, just before the Salk vaccine became available, the National Foundation for Infantile Paralysis began a program ostensibly to establish accurate polio statistics for the United States. To do this, they offered physicians a $25 fee for each reported case of polio. Unfortunately, with this kind of financial inducement, any child with a fever or a limp might very easily be reported to the foundation as presumably suffering from polio! As a result, the foundation's statistics soon demonstrated a vast epidemic of the disease.

Just as the nation was going into a panic, the vaccine was introduced. Everyone rushed their children to be vaccinated, creating millions of dollars in pharmaceutical profits. And soon, the number of polio cases did, indeed, decrease dramatically.

But much of that decrease had nothing to do with the vaccine. For one thing, the foundation stopped subsidizing reports of the illness, and this alone lowered the statistics significantly. More importantly, a semantic artifice was employed to improve the statistics even further. It is well known that approximately 50 percent of all polio infections resolve themselves within sixty days. But after the vaccine was marketed, the official definition of the disease was changed: thenceforward, symptoms could not be labeled "polio" unless they persisted more than sixty days. This action, by itself, instantly meant that 50 percent fewer people had polio. All this dramatic success in disease eradication was then duly attributed to the new vaccine.

This kind of history is important when we consider the current AIDS epidemic. Many experts fear that the reported statistics are being artificially inflated in order to assure a multibillion dollar expenditure on pharmaceuticals that may have little or no genuine value. For example, claims have been made in the United States that the heterosexual population of Africa is being decimated by AIDS. But according to an article in the *Western Journal of Medicine* for December 1987, "there are no data to support such an assertion from any AIDS-affected African countries." In addition, as already noted, according to the CDC definition nearly anything can now be defined as AIDS. The greater the number of cases the greater the panic, and this will be reflected in research grants and drug sales. The AIDS industry has become just that – a huge, billion-dollar business. And like any other enormously powerful industry, it will concentrate on further profits and it will protect itself against any threats to its continued survival and growth. When billions of dollars are at stake, actions and motives fall under highly questionable influences.

This brings me to the matter of AZT, the only drug that has been approved for the treatment of AIDS, at a cost of between three thousand and ten thousand dollars per patient, per year. AZT is actually a fairly *old* drug. It was originally developed as a treatment for cancer, but was found to be so minimally effective and so lethally toxic that it was never allowed into use. But when AIDS studies were conducted with homosexuals in the 1980s, it was approved for sale more rapidly than any drug in the FDA's history.

AZT is meant to stop the replication of HIV viruses and thus to slow down the fatal progress of AIDS. However, there is no conclusive evidence that the HIV virus is replicating during the course of illness, and the assumption that AIDS is necessarily, inevitably fatal is based on poor, distorted evidence. AZT does have certain predictable results, however. It destroys many healthy cells and causes severe anemia by destroying bone marrow. Recipients of the drug therefore need frequent blood transfusions (a procedure that itself is extremely immunosuppressive). Half of all AIDS patients cannot tolerate the drug at all; the rest can only stay on it for a limited amount of time.

What, then, is the justification for its use? According to Dr. Anthony Fauci, director of the National Institute of Allergy and Infectious Diseases (who is in charge of federal AIDS funding),

> the reason that only one drug has been made available – AZT – is because it is the only drug that has been shown in scientifically controlled trials to be safe and effective. It isn't a question of there are a lot of drugs around and only one is being released. That is the only one that has been shown to be effective.[5]

Let us briefly examine the two major claims being made here:

1. *AZT has been proven safe and effective in scientifically controlled trials.*

AZT is far from safe; it is one of the most toxic drugs ever devised. In addition to the severe anemia and immunosuppression it causes, numerous studies report extensive liver, kidney, and neurological damage caused by administration of the drug. And its effectiveness is clearly questionable, since the "scientifically controlled trials" *never took place.*[6] During the supposedly "double-blind" tests, participants quickly ascertained (by taste, or by going to a chemistry lab) whether they had been given real AZT or a placebo. Many of those on placebo then "traded" for the genuine article, unwilling to be left out of any slim hope that the drug might work. Also, many test participants, against all standards of research protocol, were simultaneously taking various other drugs and treatments. Other examples of possible tampering include allegations of statistical manipulation, allegations that records were altered, allegations of financial collusion between government agencies and pharmaceutical concerns, and even allegations that the sickest patients were deliberately given placebos in order to inflate the number of AZT "successes." These many allegations, which have all remained unanswered and unresolved, render the AZT trials totally invalid. More than one government analyst is known to have read the reports and recommended that AZT not be approved. It is unfair and irresponsible to use the results of second-rate science as justification for the promotion of a dangerous chemical.

2. *There are no other drugs available.*

The FDA has various procedural schedules for testing and approving drugs. Other, safer, drugs have been specifically placed on the slow track for approval, thus assuring AZT's continued sanctity as the only available medical treatment. Not at all incidentally, the FDA's original mandate was simply to protect the American public by determining the safety of food and drugs. While it has never achieved this goal, it has instead gone on to grant itself the added right to determine pharmaceutical "efficacy." As Raymond Brown, M.D., notes, "Proof of efficacy, like proof of virtue, is difficult at best to obtain, largely dependent on the eye (and the emotional and mental biases) of the beholder." Brown continues:

American medicine lacks many good products and therapies available in other countries, as the majority of FDA decisions concerning drugs are made by bureaucrats who have never practiced medicine . . . Oriented to large industry, the FDA has totally eliminated small innovative pharmaceutical houses by imposing impossible financial and testing demands on them . . . The agency's close ties to industry, from which FDA officials are frequently drawn, and to which they return following government service, have produced FDA leniency toward safety standards for many industry products.[7]

One final point regarding the availability of drugs: although the press reported some time ago that the FDA was willing to allow private importation and use of several as yet unapproved AIDS drugs, an FDA memo to U.S. Customs agents soon called these reports "highly exaggerated," and agents were told to make no changes in policy.

In spite of all the data available on AZT, doctors have increasingly prescribed the drug. It is now being given to people with no symptoms whatsoever, simply on the basis of a positive HIV-antibody test. The presence of an antibody means that your body has responded appropriately to a threat; yet these people are being told by authorities to take a lethal chemical for "prevention." In fact, at least one expert on record has suggested that all "high-risk" people should buy and take AZT immediately, regardless of their total lack of symptoms and perfectly normal blood tests.

In August 1989, AZT's manufacturer, the Burroughs-Wellcome company, issued a press release announcing that AZT had now been "proven" effective in preventing HIV-positive individuals from ever contracting AIDS. The research was conducted by the same scientists who conducted the original AZT trials. This claim was duly reported in the national media, which instantly accepted it as fact, even though the data, results, and conclusions of the study had not been published. Despite the fact that there had been no peer review procedure nor any chance for the scientific community or the concerned public to examine the alleged evidence, Burroughs-Wellcome's stock quickly shot up more than thirty points as millions of additional AZT prescriptions began to be filled. But solid scientific research and development are not supposed to be conducted by corporate press release. As the prestigious British medical journal *The Lancet* noted, "The US results seem exciting and may support the use of zidovudine [AZT] in early stages of HIV infection. However, it is very difficult to assess the enthusiastic press releases properly as we have not seen the data to support them." Finally, in April 1990, a partial report was published in *The New England Journal of Medicine* filled with circular logic and statistical manipulation.[8] The data showed some evidence that AZT has a reasonable preventive effect against one AIDS-related illness, PCP. However, there are several other drugs available to protect against this particular form of pneumonia, and these drugs are far safer, cheaper, and more effective. The study showed no evidence whatsoever that AZT had any significant effect on any other symptom of AIDS. As *The Lancet* editorial concluded: "In HIV infection the enormous pressure to find a successful therapy should not diminish the need for good scientific data and proper analysis of trials."[9]

First the numbers are inflated, then a single drug is promoted for billions of dollars in profits. Already, now, the word is getting out that the epidemic is not reaching the once-predicted proportions. Soon the official definition of AIDS will no doubt be narrowed down, and we will be told that thanks to medical research the epidemic is subsiding.

The AIDS crisis, while far from being over, *is* subsiding, but not because of pharmaceutical drugs. It is subsiding because people with AIDS are learning its true lessons and are learning to take care of themselves. They are learning about drug-free lifestyles, safe sex, safe environments, good nutrition, and healthy emotional and spiritual lives. They are finding the courage to change, to take responsibility for themselves, and to take responsibility for the human race. I have worked with many AIDS patients in my practice, and nowhere are people more fiercely alive, more passionately committed to personal growth and social responsibility. It is this commitment that is eventually going to bring about the end of this epidemic, and it may even help destroy the greed that the epidemic has been feeding.

The constant media repetition that "all AIDS patients will die" is a falsehood that has a powerful and dangerous hypnotic effect upon the public, upon doctors, and upon patients. The reason this universal death-sentence has been assumed, is because the disease proved fatal to the earliest victims. But the people in those studies were already close to death's door due to hepatitis and other liver diseases, drug abuse and addiction, scores of venereal diseases, severe malnutrition, and virtually every other possible factor of immune destruction. The fact that they died can not be legitimately extrapolated to presume that all AIDS patients will die. That is not what the evidence suggests. This kind of media sensationalism is poor science and poor common sense.

Not too long ago we believed that in penicillin we had discovered "the" cure for syphilis, and that we would be through with this scourge forever. We now have a new and rapidly spreading syphilis epidemic in America, brought about by drug-resistant strains we cannot control. Similarly, studies already report viruses becoming resistant to AZT, in a matter of months rather than years, and we can barely begin to imagine the terror this forebodes in terms of possible future infections and diseases. AZT, it must certainly be understood, is not the magic bullet. But it is even more crucially important that we at last come to grips with the understanding that there can be no such thing as a magic bullet. The intellectually naive attempt to find a simple, one-dimensional solution to a complex, multidimensional problem has never worked before and has now become far too dangerous to continue pursuing. Linear thinking must give way to holistic thinking, and orthodox health care must give way to holistic health care.

Like every disease, AIDS comes about from a three-way blending of *active* agents that may include various germs, actions, and poisons, a *receptivity* born of chronic, abusive health habits and life-style factors, all of which have been allowed, encouraged, and *reconciled* by our dangerous negative attitudes toward life, health, each other, and the planetary environment. To heal the human race of AIDS, we are going to have to confront all three corners of this triad.

By far the most important thing to be said about acquired immunodeficiency syndrome is that there is no such thing as a final proof that any illness is necessarily permanent or fatal. All there are, are statistics—and statistics are notoriously subject to differing interpretations. Someone's statistical analysis may gloomily conclude that as many as 99 percent of all cases end badly. But it is always possible to become the remaining 1 percent. As we shall see in Part 2, we have at our disposal the means to do just that. This is our birthright! Like Jacob's brother Esau, we can despise our birthright and sell it for the sake of a little shortsighted comfort. Or, like Jacob, we can take hold of it tightly, using all the cleverness, determination, and cunning at our disposal, fully aware that we may be forced to defend it in battle with angels.

We do not have to do so. And there are powerful influences to prevent us from daring so much—from the doom-ridden sensationalism of the media to the paternal authoritarianism of the medical establishment. But Jacob didn't listen to the authorities who told him he could not have his birthright; he didn't go along with anyone else's rules or anyone else's expectations. His story illustrates the fact that the birthright of a human being is never a guarantee, but that each one of us has a right to it if we are willing to claim it and to fight for it.

AIDS patients who have achieved control of their disease are seldom found in the clinics and programs of research centers from which reports and official statistics on AIDS originate. These patients usually attend private physicians who cooperate with them in exploring avenues of reasonable therapy and who treat all aspects of their disease.[10]

This is how AIDS, cancer, and all our diseases must be confronted; and many brave men and women who are doing so are in fact surviving. I myself have seen numerous cases of people with AIDS surviving with few or no symptoms for eight or more years, who are still defying the statistics and are still doing well. These people know that nothing is more dangerous, more ethically outrageous, or more blatantly false than to tell them that they have to die. The press sells its papers—and too many health professionals maintain a sense of control—by proclaiming the inevitability of other people's deaths. And all too often the uninformed, bullied patients accept the decision stoically and go home to die.

Surely we are all going to die one day, and death is therefore not a failure. But we *are* a failure if we do not live our own lives while we are here. If you are sick, don't let anyone tell you it is hopeless. Too many people have never learned to distinguish between "false hope" and intelligent, reasonable, determined hope. Forget the dire predictions.

Jacob won his battle with the angel. Not all of us will. But all of us, regardless of what anyone else presumes to say about our chances, can at least go out and fight for our own aims, our own wishes, and our own lives.

PART 2

THE TRIAD OF HEALING

The process of healing is threefold. It requires an active component, a receptive component, and a conciliating component.
When these three components blend properly, the result is
called healing.

But this is not to say that we really know what healing *is*, or
how the body does it. We can talk with a certain amount of
knowledge about healing, as about anything sacred, but this does
not mean that we understand its essence. The actual healing
itself is a mystery. (Since the healing of a living being is so
intimately related to life and death, it could hardly be otherwise.)

Still, we are faced by the possibility – and probably the moral
duty – to aid the healing process when possible, by enhancing
one or more of the three component forces. Since we are, after all,
approaching a mystery, we have to be on guard not to inadver-
tently distort rather than enhance: the primary rule of any healing art has always been "First, do no harm." One accidental way
to distort these forces is to overestimate our abilities. The most
dangerous way of all is not really to care about the patient.

In the following three chapters I shall discuss the healing arts,
healthy customs and habits, and the healing role of the human
psyche. But I do not mean to imply that these elements themselves
are the three forces of healing. They are only attempts to be of
service to them. We may see a reflection of these forces in a smooth-
ly running body, but this is only a reflection of something ineffable.

3

Active Healing:
The Healing Arts

A healing art, like any art, is a product of the knowledge, wishes, and beliefs of the people and culture within which it develops. Those who believe that the phenomena of the physical world are due to the whims of unseen gods will train their doctors in the art of appeasing those gods. Those who believe that the world is created and maintained by the action of conflicting supernatural forces will develop a healing art based on the harmony of these forces. Those who place their belief in science will develop a scientific healing art. A remarkable finding of countless psychological and anthropological studies is that every one of these different systems has a reasonably high rate of success among those people for whom it makes sense.

THE WESTERN TRADITION

Our Western healing tradition began when Hippocrates declared that all diseases are explainable by discernible laws of nature. The Greek explanation of nature at that time was based on principles of earth, water, air, and fire. (This explanation had various levels of meaning, from the physical to the psychological to the divine, but on the most basic level we can see that earth, water, air, and fire are directly analogous to solid, liquid, gas, and energy, the forms of matter we still talk about in modern science). Hippocrates took this fourfoldedness of the macrocosm and applied it to man, the microcosm. Man, he said, contained four "humors": blood, phlegm, black bile, and yellow bile. Illness resulted when these humors got out of balance with each other.

To help heal his patients, Hippocrates attempted to balance the humors by using herbs, exercise, and diet.

The theory of Hippocrates was derived from philosophical speculation coupled with his direct observations of the visibly obvious. Such an approach may also convince us, for example, that the earth is in the center of the universe. Given this latter belief, Aristotle developed a reasonable explanation for most visible phenomena: for example, tossed objects fall back to earth because the natural place of solid objects is in the center of all things; the natural place of water is in a region, or shell, surrounding the central shell of earth—which explains why lakes and seas float upon the surface of the earth; the shell of air surrounds that of water; and the stars remain in the sky, and flames leap upward, because the natural place of fire is in the fourth, outermost shell. Aristotle's laws of physics were based on the reasonable belief that things have an inherent tendency to seek their natural place.

The Aristotelian system is actually quite practical. It offers a coherent explanation of most observable events in the world, and can be used to accurately predict many future physical events. When Copernicus declared that the earth was not in the center of the universe (implying, as he did so, that our observations of the visibly obvious cannot always be trusted), a whole new science of physics had to be developed to explain why things happened the way they did. This monumental task was undertaken in the seventeenth century by Isaac Newton, who developed the system of mechanical physics that eventually led to the industrial revolution and ultimately to the birth of modern technology. None of this could have come about if it had not been for a French philosopher, René Descartes, who persuasively argued that the "world" and "I" are totally distinct entities—a radically new idea at the time—and it is therefore possible for this "I" to observe external, worldly phenomena objectively (that is, without including oneself as *part* of the phenomena), and to conduct objective, empirical, scientific experiments *upon* this external world.

Our Western tradition now had a new framework of belief. Questions about nature (including questions about health) were henceforward approached quantitatively, rather than qualitatively. Experimental evidence accompanied every statement about the nature of the world—a world totally unconnected to the inner life of the observer. Theories were proposed only after an accumulation of empirical data, and in accordance with this data. The scientific tradition was thus born—interestingly enough, on the basis of one rather wobbly premise. Aristotle had said that things fall back to earth because that is where things belong. Since the earth was no longer in the center of the universe, his theory could no longer apply. But things still continued to fall back to earth! In light of the new Copernican cosmology, a new explanation was needed. The answer Newton gave was that all pieces of matter attract each other by an intrinsic attractive principle—which amounts to saying nothing more than that things attract each other because they attract each other! This dubious explanation, called "gravity," is the necessary key to all of Newton's formidable principles of universal mechanics. Newton himself acknowledged that it was a totally unsatisfactory answer, and even our best modern theories have so far failed to give a completely satisfactory explanation of why a ball, thrown into the air, always comes down again.

With the new scientific outlook, and the complementary explanations and predictions of mechanical physics, the Copernican revolution was complete. Newton's mathematical work was without precedent. With his formulas he and his successors could explain and predict the motions and reactions of everything on earth and everything in the sky. The universe, including the human body, now appeared as a smooth-running machine, following clear physical laws with no exceptions. Everything from the body to the mind to the earth to the galaxies could now be understood in terms of little material particles and simple laws of motion. In Western thought, the theory of determinism now reigned.

"But it was of the greatest consequence for succeeding thought," writes E. A. Burtt in *The Metaphysical Foundations of Modern Physical Science,* that now the great Newton's authority was squarely behind that view of the cosmos which saw in man a puny, irrelevant specta- tor . . . of the vast mathematical system whose regular motions, according to mechanical principles, constituted the world of na- ture. The gloriously romantic universe of Dante and Milton, that set no bounds to the imagination of man as it played over space and time, had now been swept away. . . . The world that people thought themselves living in – a world rich with color and sound, redolent with fragrance, filled with gladness, love and beauty, speaking everywhere of purposive harmony and creative ideals – is crowded now into minute corners in the brains of scattered organic beings. The really important world outside was a world hard, cold, colorless and dead: a world of quantity, a world of mathematically computable motions in mechanical regularity.[1]

Within this Newtonian framework, a Newtonian healing art was needed in which we could also believe. The "old" medicine saw in both man and the universe a play of eternal and divine forces: things went well when these forces were in harmony, and they went badly when this harmony was disturbed. The "new" medicine, taking its cue from empirical, quantitative sci- ence, saw in man the mechanical interplay of separate pieces of matter, and began to look at diseases as specific, discrete entities, irrelevant of the person who happened to contract them – and it began to seek specific remedies for each specific illness. In this pursuit, it turned to the traditions of the herbalists. But the approach was quite different. The herbalist listens to the patient in a "holistic" way, believing that the patient is not distinct from the illness, and thus looks for a total picture of the situation: symptoms, history, life-style, beliefs, feelings, wishes, habits, and so forth. He or she then puts together a combination of herbs that fits the individual pattern. The herbalist deals with the complexities of the whole patient, and with the *synergistic* quali- ties of nature's various remedies. Scientific medicine, by con- trast, seeks to extract individual and particular ingredients *from* nature's remedies, and to use them separately as specific agents to fight specific, isolatable disease entities that have invaded specific, isolatable parts of mechanical bodies. The "old" medicine worked slowly, at the level of the organs, cooperating with their inherent, interconnected processes. The "new" medicine sought to bypass the organs and go straight to the level of our cells and molecules. Events move much more quickly on this level, and this new medicine could thus effect changes much more rapidly and dramatically.

In the nineteenth century, when pneumonia, syphilis, and tuberculosis were rampant, the possibility of a rapid and effective means for attacking disease still seemed a distant miracle, but one that was just beginning to seem possible, due to the explanation of Louis Pasteur that microscopically small organisms were at the root of many diseases, and the theoretical possibility that we could find some means to destroy them without simultaneously killing the patient. In the meantime, as Lewis Thomas notes, "the medical literature of those years makes horrifying reading today: paper after learned paper recounts the benefits of bleeding, cupping, violent purging, the raising of blisters by vesicant ointments, the immersion of the body in either ice water or intolerably hot water."[2] Most of these actions did more harm than good.

In response to the reckless and often deadly methods of nineteenth-century medicine, two alternative approaches to healing were developed in the United States, both of which took the patient's musculoskeletal structure as a starting point: chiropractic and osteopathy. These two healing arts were a response to a terrible situation, and they revived an ancient tradition of human touch and physical manipulation as a means of safely stimulating the body to heal. To Hippocrates himself is attributed the saying, "Get knowledge of the spine, for this is the requisite for many diseases."

As practitioners of medicine became aware of the dangers and futility of most of their treatments, they turned instead to a more reserved, safe, in-depth study of *diagnosis*, based on the principle of the specific, separate, impersonal disease entity. By the turn of the nineteenth century and well into the twentieth, medical doctors viewed their main task as trying to identify disease, to predict its course, and to comfort the patient while the disease took that course. Speaking of his own medical training in the

1930s, Lewis Thomas recounts that the purpose of the curriculum "was to teach the recognition of disease entities, their classification, their signs, symptoms, and laboratory manifestations, and how to make an accurate diagnosis. The treatment of disease was the most minor part of the curriculum, almost left out altogether."[3]

LOSSES AND GAINS OF MODERN MEDICINE

Into this task came technology, and the diagnostic skills of Western medicine became truly profound. Here, however, as medicine gained on one front, it also began to lose one of its finest qualities, as Thomas has pointed out:

> Today, the doctor can perform a great many of his most essential tasks from his office in another building without ever seeing the patient. There are even computer programs for the taking of a history. . . . Instead of spending forty-five minutes listening to the chest and palpating the abdomen, the doctor can sign a slip which sends the patient off to the X-ray department for a CT scan, with the expectation of seeing within the hour, in exquisite detail, all the body's internal organs. . . . The doctor can set himself, if he likes, at a distance, remote from the patient and his family, never touching anyone beyond a perfunctory handshake at the first and only contact.[4]

This loss is not just important for sentimental reasons. Human contact and human touch have been shown to be a critical part of the healing process. They may, indeed, have nothing to do with a specific attack on a specific disease entity. But it is not the entity that must heal—it is the *patient* who must heal. In his excellent book on the healing arts, Ted Kaptchuk makes a distinction between "disease" (an objective condition, comparable to what I keep referring to as the specific, separate, disease entity, which really has nothing to do with the individual patient), and "illness" (which Kaptchuk defines as the state of the patient as felt and perceived by the patient).[5] Studies have shown that animals under great stress will wither and die, but if they are periodically petted and gentled, they will produce higher levels of adrenal hormones and will survive much longer. Young mammals kept from the touch of their mothers (even if allowed to see her and hear her, and even when fed well and cared for in other respects), become violent and self-destructive. Further, as Ashley Montagu states in his classic study *Touching*, "The mounting evidence that the skin has an immunologic function has recently been confirmed by a number of independent investigators." Elsewhere in the same book, Montagu relates the following incident, which took place in a Boston hospital a few short decades ago:

> The wards were very neat and tidy, but what piqued Dr. Talbot's curiosity was the sight of a fat old woman who was carrying a very measly baby on her hip. "Who's that?" inquired Dr. Talbot. "Oh, that," replied Schlossman, "is Old Anna. When we have done everything we can medically for a baby, and it is still not doing well, we turn it over to Old Anna, and she is always successful."[6]

Western scientific medicine has chosen to move further and further away from the patient, and closer and closer to the patient's disease. Other healing arts, such as chiropractic, osteopathy, herbalism, and homeopathy, have continued to work alongside the whole patient. Approached from this vantage point, all of the healing arts can be seen as complementary to each other, rather than being opposed to each other or in competition with each other. The various nonmedical healing arts can be seen as necessary attempts to preserve some of the finer, more human, qualitatively essential elements of healing—important aspects of our lives that none of us really want to lose. And given the intense animosity that organized medicine has always directed toward them in the United States, it is a tribute to their value and rationality that they have all survived.

In fact, since medicine's task until recently had little to do with actually treating anything, it might have been relegated to a secondary role as a purely diagnostic art of limited practical importance. But then something momentous happened. After years of perseverance, researchers at last discovered certain specific agents that were actually able to attack specific diseases! First came a cure for syphilis, then came the sulfa drugs, and soon came penicillin and the whole variety of antibiotics. Some years earlier, Pasteur had explained the function of tiny germs in initiating disease. Now, at last, these germs could be destoyed and health restored, as Paul de Kruif discusses in his classic *Microbe Hunters:*

Came 1910, and that was Paul Ehrlich's year. One day, that year, he walked into the scientific congress at Koenigsberg, and there was applause. . . . He told of how the magic bullet had been found at last. He told of the terror of the disease of the loathsome name [syphilis], of those sad cases that went to horrible disfiguring death, or to what was worse—the idiot asylums. One shot [of Ehrlich's new drug, called "606" because it was the six hundred and sixth compound he tried after many grueling years of experimentation] and they were up, they were on their feet, they gained thirty pounds. It was biblical, no less. It was miraculous—no drug nor herb of the old women and priests and medicine men of the ages had ever done tricks like that. . . . Never was there such applause.[7]

Indeed, medicine could perform miracles unlike anything else. Modern science at last had its scientific healing art. And it has changed the lives of us all ever since.

From drugs that combat infectious diseases, to microsurgical techniques for reconnecting severed limbs, to the invention of artificial hearts, the power of modern Western medicine cannot be overestimated, nor the debt we owe its researchers. But is this the whole story? "Because we have all experienced the uncertainties of being a patient and the relief of healing," writes Dr. Kaptchuk,

we assume that modern medicine has found the causes of disease and thus is responsible for the extension of our lives and our sense of being well. Yet this is a widespread fallacy on two levels. First, because of the placebo effect and other aspects of the healing process . . . a high percentage of illness is relieved regardless of medications; Second, and more important, the provision of adequate food, clean water, and proper sanitation has reduced or eliminated the great killer diseases throughout the world independently of modern drugs. . . . This is not meant to decry the value of antibiotics, which accelerated the decline of infections, or of other achievements of modern medicine such as the spectacular interventions of surgery. Rather, it is meant to put scientific medicine's achievements in a realistic perspective."[8]

Cardiovascular disease, chronic inflammatory diseases of all sorts, and cancer are far from being conquered because we have not yet put medicine into perspective with nutrition and exercise, environmental safety, psychological and spiritual health, and the other significant healing arts. Medical advances have extended our lives, but by remaining in a vacuum, modern medicine has been unable to sufficiently improve the *quality* of our lives.

THE LIMITATIONS OF SCIENCE

Let us take one more step and put science itself into perspective. To do this, consider for a moment what science can and cannot tell us about our faculty of sight.

The miracle of "seeing" is fascinating, and at first consideration it is marvelously simple. A ray of light bounces off a nearby object and passes into the eye. First it traverses a lens, which, according to well-known laws of optics, turns the light ray upside down and focuses it on the back wall of the eye chamber. This inner wall is covered with tiny nerve endings that connect directly to the large optic nerve. These nerve endings (the so-called rods and cones) are stimulated by the energy of the inverted light ray that has just entered, and they respond by sending electrical messages down the optic nerve to deep within the brain. Here the multitude of nerve cells that make up the brain's "visual area" receive these electrical messages and react with a flurry of electrical activity of their own. Viewing this activity on a deeper biophysical level, we can say that the various electrons, protons, and neutrons that make up these brain cells respond to the incoming electrical impulses by changing their positions and rates of vibration. And then we see.

And then we see.

When? When the atoms start to vibrate differently? But we do not see vibrating atoms. We see an object "out there"—an intangible image of a tangible tree, a chair, or a lover's face. What does this have to do with vibrating atoms in my skull? What is the link? What bridges the gap between vibrating atoms and the image that I see? Nothing in the realm of science could ever bridge that gap. Does the above anatomical-physiological description really explain anything?

The pattern is familiar: as science gets closer and closer to the specific physical events that "make up" sight, it gets further and further away from the total experience of sight itself. In fact we do not know what sight is. We know that it is accompanied by certain events in the physical body, events that can be observed, measured, quantified, labeled, and even predicted with great accuracy. But that is all we know. As far as the actual phenomenon that we call "seeing" is concerned, science can explain nothing.

An interesting corollary to this fact is that since science does not know what seeing *is,* and since the primary function of a scientist is to "observe" (i.e., to "see"), then science clearly is unable to explain scientifically what it is doing. This serious logical flaw in its own internal system tells us much about the inadvisability of depending on science as our only legitimate means of studying the world. There are two excesses to be avoided, warned the great seventeenth-century mathematician and philosopher Blaise Pascal: to exclude rational thinking, and to admit nothing but rational thinking. "Reason's last step," he said, "is the recognition that there are an infinite number of things which are beyond it. It is merely feeble if it does not go as far as to realize that."[9].

A good deal of information is available to us today about the physics of light and electricity, along with some anatomical and biochemical facts about the brain. On the basis of this knowledge, we can accomplish extraordinary feats in such fields as medicine and technology. But the point here is neither the brilliance of the discoveries that science has already made, nor the magnitude of knowledge that is yet to be obtained. Nor is the point in any way to downgrade the importance of scientific work or scientific knowledge. The point is simply to make very clear that when science has learned everything it can possibly learn about eyes and brains and electrical energy, it will still not be able to explain what sight is. It may ultimately be able to give a complete description of the biological, chemical, and physical events that simultaneously occur when we see, but the miracle itself will remain outside its understanding.

This is not because there is anything wrong with science. It is because of the very essence of what science is all about. *Science is descriptive only. It ultimately explains nothing.* Science asks the question "how?" This question is both practically important and intellectually fascinating. But we must recognize that it is not the concern of science to ask "why?" "Why?" is an emotional and spiritual question as well as an intellectual one, and it can only be approached with just this sort of balanced human reason. We may never be able to answer it fully, but the dignity of men and women – what makes it possible for us to be different from other creatures – lies in our individual concern with this question.

When the purpose and limitations of science are understood, the pursuit of science becomes very beautiful. When not understood, the worship of science becomes very dangerous. To pronounce with utter certainty that something has been "proven scientifically" and must therefore be unquestionably accepted as absolutely and inarguably true, is inconsistent with the meaning of science itself as well as with human reason.

When medicine says that germs cause disease, it is talking about one important active cause. But this oversimplification ignores the equally important receptive and conciliatory causes, as well as the great multiplicity of active causes. Pasteur himself, on his deathbed, acknowledged that germs were not the only consideration in disease, or even the primary one. He said that the condition of the patient's body, the ability to fight off or succumb to the action of a germ, was more important than the germ itself. "Microbes are nothing," he is reported to have said; "the soil is everything."

Disease is a mistake. It means that the natural order of things has gone awry. Why? Why do diseases occur? Medicine does not ask this question. What medicine does ask is:

1. What abnormal processes occur when a patient is sick?
2. What can be done to relieve the symptoms, and to halt these damaging processes?

These are not unimportant questions. They are *extremely important* questions. But other questions also need to be addressed:

1. Why does disease occur in the first place?
2. What can be done to keep this from occurring and recurring?

Other healing arts do consider these questions. The conflict between orthodox medicine and holistic healing systems is based on the mistaken notion that practitioners of the two systems are trying to do the same thing by using different methods. For instance, the notion is that medical doctors try to cure cancer with drugs and radiation, whereas holistic practitioners try to cure cancer with vitamins and acupuncture needles. But this is not the case. Not only are the methods different; the purpose is also different. One group is trying to fight the terrible *effects* of disease; the second group is trying to rectify the problems that *allow* for disease. In a sane world we would be working together, not indulging in pointless enmity. As Ted Kaptchuk notes,

> every healing art sees illness in its own terms. Patients need to remember that the illness is theirs and theirs alone. . . . Once we awaken from the dogmatic slumber of believing that one medicine has all the answers, then we can go on with an open mind to examine the whole range of healing systems that the genius of the human race has so patiently worked out.[10]

COMPLEMENTARY HEALING ARTS

Chiropractic

Medical science observes the distortion of body function by an active agent and then uses drugs or surgery either to counter that agent or to replace the body's own active function, even if deleterious side effects are sometimes brought about as well. The approach of chiropractic, like that of other holistic arts, is not to *oppose* a distorted active force, but to *redirect* it, to remove interferences, and to encourage its appropriate action. At the same time, these healing arts stress the equal importance of healthy living habits and healthy psychological attitudes. A holistic doctor serves as a teacher, and he or she tries to help each patient to fuse a complete, personal triad of healing.

Pain is not a disease. In fact, pain is not even itself a problem. Pain is the way the body tells you that you *have* a problem. It occurs whenever tissue is being damaged. Nature is not telling you to stop the pain but to stop the damage. The pain will then take care of itself.

The analogy of a Geiger counter is very apt here. When a dangerous radioactive substance is nearby, the Geiger counter produces an irritating noise. The "solution" to the problem (of having to listen to this unpleasant noise) is not to turn off the Geiger counter, even though it may be temporarily soothing to do so. Rather, one should keep the Geiger counter on, be grateful to it, and then find and remove the radioactive substance.

When the body's nervous system sends out signals of irritation and pain, reaching for an aspirin or a Valium is just like turning off the Geiger counter. It allows you to go on placidly, without dealing with the problem. Certainly your body may take care of the problem while you ignore it; but all too often it does the reverse. Certainly there are pain levels that of themselves are potentially damaging or simply unendurable, and these must be relieved. But this is not the general rule.

Spend any day in a doctor's office, and you are sure to hear this story several times: "You know, Doc, I was fine until about three years ago when I got the flu. That went away pretty quickly with the pills I took, but then my stomach started hurting. And since then it's been one thing after another!" It turns out that with each new symptom, this patient found a way to relieve the pain. But the *problem*—which may have stemmed from emotional stress, an improperly cared-for injury, or an unhealthy diet—remained. The body is smart: if we do not listen to its first message, it will send another, and the next message may be more unpleasant. If we shut off each successive Geiger counter, it will keep broadcasting new symptoms until we listen and do something about the *problem*.

Chiropractic is a healing art that deals with one such problem area—one that is probably universal and that often causes a great deal of pain along with a general, nonspecific type of interference in normal body functioning. This interference may then become a primary contributing factor in the formation of any number of further health problems.

The nervous system controls and coordinates all the functions of the body. It is a powerful yet sensitive instrument, so nature has carefully encased the brain and spinal cord within a protective casement of bone. Rather than hold the cord in a rigid, bony tomb, thus eliminating vast possibilities of life-expressing movement, nature has created a flexible system of separate vertebrae, connected together by soft discs and ball bearing-like capsules. This system allows for all forms of motion. The spine is our support, our protection, and the source of our movement and action. It fully deserves all the connotations of the word *backbone*. It is the center of our physical being. It needs to be kept flexible and strong.

Like any part of the body, the spine may develop problems. Stress, toxic environments, or simple bad postural or dietary habits can cause muscle tensions that tug at vertebrae and distort the symmetry of the spine. The twisting and pulling that often occurs during childbirth, for example, may cause injuries to the neck that then affect the child's entire lifetime. Falling, fighting, twisting, pulling, jerks and jolts, heavy exertion, minor injuries, and all the little stresses in everyday life can and do cause vertebrae to slip out of their ideal, natural alignment and to remain stuck due to tight muscles. Such spinal distortions

- Limit our movement ability, our sense of physical freedom, openness, and expressiveness
- Often cause pain, sometimes crippling pain, by irritating nearby nerves
- Interfere with the ability of the nervous system to control all the delicate functions of the body

One job of a doctor is to assist nature by helping the patient remove anything that interferes with the natural functioning of the body. These spinal distortions, which physiology textbooks call "vertebral subluxations," are a major source of interference.

Correcting vertebral subluxations promotes a normal, unimpeded flow of information between the brain and the rest of the body. This overall improvement in alignment and communication will always allow for finer functioning of every bodily system: immune, endocrine, cardiovascular, gastrointestinal, and so on. Such alignment promotes finer adaptation and growth and a fuller use of mind and emotions. It stimulates the capacity to heal. It improves the quality of life.

Chiropractic combines the science of locating vertebral subluxations with the art of correcting them through safe, gentle manipulation. It is a fascinatingly simple healing art, concerned only with enhancing the body's own healing capabilities, and it often yields profound restorative effects. Chiropractic is not meant to serve "instead" of medicine, nor is it merely an alternative means of getting rid of backaches (although most backaches do naturally improve when the spine is properly aligned; even the American Medical Association has evidence on file that manipulation is the most effective treatment for many cases of back pain). And chiropractic is not a cure—nor does it claim to be a cure—for any disease. Rather, chiropractic is an essential and effective way of assisting nature and assisting the patient, by increasing flexibility and comfort, and by simply eliminating one of the more significant factors that interfere with normal health and healing.

Chinese Medicine

The idea of the complementarity—rather than the antagonism—of opposites plays a major role in Eastern philosophy. Out of this philosophy came a broad healing art that includes the use of diet, exercise, meditation, herbs, and acupuncture.

Since the reopening of formal relations between the United States and China in the 1970s, there has been a relatively high degree of interest on the part of the West in this form of treatment, much of it aroused by the dramatic sight of surgery being performed using only acupuncture needles to anesthetize the patient. Unfortunately, the wide coverage of such cases in the media led to the widespread misconception that the purpose and effectiveness of acupuncture is limited to pain control. A yet deeper misconception comes from our relentless drive to explain acupuncture scientifically, in terms of our Newtonian worldview. The Chinese, on the other hand, say that acupuncture works by harmonizing the energies of two basic principles called *yin* and *yang*—and since their healing art has served them so well since ancient times, it may be worth the effort to consider the Chinese explanation of acupuncture.

Acupuncture is born of three cosmological concepts: (1) Tao, (2) *yin* and *yang*, and (3) the Theory of Five Elements. *Tao* means "the Way." It is the key to the intermingling of heaven and earth. Tao is a philosophy of life, a system whereby man acknowledges and fulfills his responsibility to live in accord with natural laws. According to *The Yellow Emperor's Canon of Internal Medicine* (an ancient Chinese medical text, written in the form of a dialogue between the mythic Yellow Emperor, Huang-ti, and his teacher, Chi Po), people of a bygone era lived well beyond a hundred years because they lived in harmony with the Tao. For this reason, longevity became a symbol of sainthood.

Like Hippocrates, the Chinese evolved much of their philosophy by observing nature: the flowing changes of night and day, seasonal hot and cold, growth and decay. They also saw that if they did not live by nature's laws, nature would exact a heavy price. "The only manner in which man could attain the right Way, the Tao, was by emulating the course of the universe and complete adjustment to it," as Ilza Veith points out. "Thus man saw the universe endowed with a spirit that was indomitable in its strength and unforgiving toward disobedience."[11]

Within the universe, heavier substances sink down to form the earth, while lighter substances rise to form Heaven. The Chinese called the two components of this overall duality *yin* and *yang*. As these two divine forces interact with each other and begin to

create manifest nature, it is natural that everything *in* nature has
qualities of *yin* and *yang*. For example:

Yang has to do with	*Yin* has to do with
Heaven	Earth
Sun	Moon
Day	Night
Fire	Water
Expansion	Contraction
Light	Dark

Just as Heaven (*yang*) sends fertility (in the from of sunlight) to
the earth (*yin*), which then gives rise to life, so the relation of
heaven and earth was reflected in the relation of husband and
wife—and man was seen as representing the *yang* principle on
earth, woman the *yin* principle. Yet the ancient Chinese also
knew that there was *yin* within *yang*, and *yang* within *yin*. Neither
component ever exists alone in an absolute state.

Yin and *yang* are descriptive words. They are ever-present
qualities of everything in existence, and they describe an ever-
changing, relative, quantitative proportion between themselves.
In this dynamic universe, and within every human being, *yin*
and *yang* are forever in motion: building and destroying, growing
and decaying, fighting and reconciling—just as night gives way
to day and back to night, as the seasons change, and as men and
women relate to one another. Harmony between the two forces
means health. Disharmony, an undue preponderance of one
force, means disease. (Harmony does not mean that the amounts
of *yin* and *yang* need ever be equal.) "But man is not helplessly
exposed to the whims of Yin and Yang," notes Veith. "Man had
received the doctrine of Tao as a means of maintaining perfect
balance and to secure himself health and a long life."

As the divine forces of *yin* and *yang*, overseen by the universal
Tao, continue to evolve further and further into material nature,
their triadic, interweaving "dance" must also follow definite natural laws. Whereas *yin* and *yang* are descriptive words relating to
state, the Theory of Five Elements explains the laws that regulate
change. Change may proceed in a generative direction (toward

health, adaptation, and growth), or in a degenerative direction (toward sickness, decay, and death). Along the way, these changes (which may be physical processes, emotional processes, or cosmic processes), must always pass through five phases, or "elements," in one or another sequence. The Chinese symbolized these necessary elements of sequential changes as metal, fire, wood, water, and earth.

To understand a patient's illness, the Chinese doctor must know several things: the proportional state of *yin* and *yang* in the patient's body, particularly in those parts that are involved with the illness; the phase in which the illness finds itself and that toward which it is moving (e.g., from "wood" toward "water"). From such a profound understanding, the Chinese doctor would have a good idea of what needed to be done to bring about recovery.

In chapter 1, I referred to the fact that a wound inflicted on a dead body will never heal, no matter what steps are taken. At the first moment after death, nothing in our physiological body is any different than it was in the last moment before death. But *something* has fled. We might simply call it a life force, or some sort of life energy. The Chinese call it *ch'i*. And they have found that *ch'i* circulates through the body via pathways called "meridians."

Throughout much of Western literature and thought, the blood is seen as the symbol and essence of life. In Chinese medicine, too, blood and *ch'i* are closely related, for *ch'i* is said to be transmitted through the blood. Hence, Eastern medicine uses pulse diagnosis to analyze the amount and quality of *ch'i* that is present in the twelve meridians. Each wrist actually contains six discrete pulses that record even the most subtle changes taking place in each meridian. Pulse diagnosis, in which the doctor touches and measures the patient's pulse for minutes or even hours, is a sensitive art that may take a lifetime to perfect. The pulse serves as a basis not only for diagnosis but also for prognosis. However, the pulse is not the only consideration. The doctor also considers color, odors, sounds, emotions, breathing, facial appearance, even dreams. This method does not diagnose a *disease:* it diagnoses a *patient*.

Once a diagnosis has been made, treatment can begin. Acupuncture is one mode of treatment. The insertion of needles into specific points along the meridians opens up blockages so that *ch'i* can flow unimpeded (just as a chiropractic spinal manipulation opens up different blockages so that nerve energy can flow unimpeded). Specifically, the needles do one of three things: (1) tonify a meridian that is *deficient* in *ch'i* (such a deficiency might lead, for instance, to symptoms of weakness or fatigue); (2) sedate a meridian that has an *excess* of *ch'i* (excess might lead to such conditions as fever, inflammation, etc.); or (3) disperse *ch'i* that has become *stagnant* (causing, perhaps, a lingering cold, a lump in the throat, or some other symptom that is "stuck" in the patient).

Acupuncture is not the only form of treatment, of course. The traditional teacher Chi Po tells the Yellow Emperor that there are five aspects to treatment:

> The first method cures the spirit; the second gives knowledge of how to nourish the body; the third gives knowledge of the true effects of poisons and medicines; the fourth explains acupuncture and the use of the small and large needle; the fifth tells how to examine and treat the intestines and viscera, the blood and the breath.[12]

Meditation and contemplation on the Tao; ingestion of nutritious foods, herbs, and medicines; the practice of *t'ai chi;* acupuncture; fasting; and (rarely) the use of surgery: these are the healing methods of Chinese medicine.

Chinese medicine takes full account of the fact that we complex humans are physical, sexual, emotional, psychological, social, and spiritual beings. "It embodies the experience of an old and great people in wrestling with the problems of mortal ills and the preservation of human health. It indicates the closest possible integration between moral and physical conduct, and is therefore an early adumbration of the relationship between mental and physical states of health."[13]

Homeopathy

Another art that traces its theoretical roots back to Hippocrates, homeopathic medicine is a system actually developed by one man, Samuel Hahnemann, a German physician. Horrified at the excesses of nineteenth-century medicine, Hahnemann recalled that Hippocrates' original use of poisonous substances had been tempered according to a principle of refinement. He therefore embarked on a search for the development of "safe" medicine.

Quinine, an extract of cinchona bark, was being used at that time as a treatment for malaria. Hahnemann, who was perfectly healthy, ingested some of this curative tree bark and developed some of the symptoms of malaria. From this experience, he hypothesized that a substance that can cure a sick person may cause the same symptoms in a well person. He and his followers, over many decades, tested and demonstrated this theory repeatedly by experimenting on themselves with various substances. For example, they found that if over a period of time a healthy person is given continuous doses of the leaves of the white cedar tree, a variety of symptoms will begin to develop: the skin will become waxy; itching and burning of mucous membrane will occur; the subject becomes irritable and quarrelsome; headaches may occur; urination becomes painful and more frequent; most symptoms tend to be worse at night.

It is remarkable to look back and realize that homeopathic pioneers discovered this information by experimenting on themselves and by keeping intensive personal records of every new sensation, emotion, or thought that they experienced. The *Materia Medica* of homeopathy consists of volumes of information on the results of these human experiments. Some substances have been shown to produce the stated effects in hundreds of cases, and are now used as standard remedies. Some substances are listed with the results of just a few experiments, and are considered possible remedies needing further verification. They are called "remedies" because of Hahnemann's original discovery— that if a substance can produce a particular "symptomatic picture" in a healthy person, then it is likely to cure a sick person who has developed these same symptoms. This principle is referred to by the Latin term *similia similibus curantur*, which simply means "like cures like."

What especially excited Hahnemann in his search for a safe form of treatment was the observation that a patient with all the symptoms produced by white cedar leaves could be cured by taking a minute, harmless dose of the leaves. In fact, as his research continued he found that the smaller the dose, the more potent the healing effect! This was not an immediate conclusion, however. At first, Hahnemann kept lowering the dosage in order to avoid the problem of side effects, and as a result not very much happened. He then claims to have discovered something very peculiar, something that has made homeopathy a bit of a laughingstock in the eyes of orthodox practitioners. The key, Hahnemann claimed, was first to dilute the substance to the tiniest possible dosage, and then to shake it violently. This shaking was what "potentized" the remedy, making it even more powerful than a large dose of the undiluted substance.

Medical scientists could find no coherent explanation for such a claim, and therefore sought to debunk it. The disbelief got even worse as Hahnemann began to dilute his remedies to such an extent that, according to the laws of chemistry and the law of averages, not one single molecule of the original substance could be left. And these were considered the strongest remedies! Soon, as conventional medicine became less excessive and more effective, the strange inexplicable art of homeopathy fell out of favor and all but disappeared.

Today, however, homeopathy is experiencing a renaissance. Alarmed by the side effects of drugs, radiation, and other toxic and dangerous medical treatments, many people are looking once again for "safe" medicines. Interest in homeopathy is increasing. "Admittedly, to anyone confronted for the first time with this material, it may sound fantastic or even incredible," notes Dr. Edward Whitmont. "Yet, since it is the result of repeated controlled experiments, it could be rejected only upon the evidence of similar experiments, under the same rigid conditions, which would fail to produce those results. To the best of the writer's knowledge, any such *experimental* refutation has never taken place."[14] Medical science has always sought to discredit its homeopathic competition not because it has in any way disproved its efficacy but because it has never figured out how it works. And the most important justification for homeopathy is that, according to the testimony of thousands upon thousands of patients, it often *does* work.

At the same time, we do have to wonder why homeopathy works. If we can understand why a healing art works, we may be able to build upon it even further and make it even more useful. It may be useful, too, to remove our questions from the context of the old Newtonian mechanical science. Somewhere in the theories of modern physics – which tell us that matter and energy are only different ways of looking at the same thing – we might find a clue as to why the energetic shaking of minute amounts of matter has a "potentizing" effect. An even more productive context may be the world of quantum physics, which has shown us that everything, be it energy or matter, in its very essence is nothing more than "vibration." Since everything is vibration, it is logical to conclude that in a state of health each of our organs must have a certain, normal, overall-appropriate *type* of vibration, which in theory we ought to be able to use as a kind of "signature" for that particular organ, and which is nothing more than a summation of all the normal vibrations of all the healthy cells, atoms, and particles that together make up the particular organ. In a state of disease, the very misbehavior of the organ indicates that its components are not functioning properly – and on the most fundamental level, what these components "do" is to *vibrate*. Disease, at least in part, must mean that they are vibrating wrongly. If there were some way to measure the abnormal vibrational rates of our organs, cells, and atoms, we would of course have a most powerful form of diagnosis. If we could then learn all the laws of appropriate natural vibration, we would have a profound understanding of health. And if we could then devise a means of *restoring* the appropriate type of vibration to the various parts of our bodies, we would have the ultimate healing art for the age of quantum physics.

Perhaps, in some otherwise inexplicable way, this is what psychic healers do when they lay their hands on a patient and transmit what they call "healing energy." Transmitting such energies and affecting internal vibrations is certainly what the American Indians were attempting to do when they used crystals for healing purposes. It is also the basis for the healing effects of such interesting fields as "sound therapy" and "color therapy." And it is probably the basis for the physical healing effects of certain forms of visualization and meditation. Finally, it is the most likely explanation for the efficacy of a homeopathic remedy. Medicine would be correct in the statement that a homeopathic remedy cannot possibly do anything, if what they mean by this statement is that a homeopathic remedy cannot do anything *material:* that is, it cannot do anything mechanical to any material body tissue. Medicine deals with chemistry, but it does not deal with the subtle vibrational energies of the chemicals. It deals on the useful level of their mechanical interactions with each other, but one step deeper is a level of internal energetic vibrations. Only radiation therapy makes any connection to this world of vibrations, and it does so in the form of a desperate, blustering attack, with as yet no knowledge of how this attack accomplishes what it does, and with serious, often fatal, side effects. Homeopathic remedies, even those that apparently do not have a single molecule left of their original base substance, might possibly be functioning on the level of restoring our biophysical vibrations to normal by using a principle of resonance, rather than a principle of attack.

A REEMERGING WORLDVIEW

Certain specific and definitive assumptions about the essence of space, time, matter, and energy are necessary and fundamental to Newtonian physics, scientific medicine, and philosophical materialism, and also underlie the "common sense" of today. Here are a few examples: the shortest distance between two points is always a straight line; parallel lines never meet; if I have just seen ten seconds elapse on my clock, then no one ought to be able to prove that only eight seconds have elapsed. These statements are "obvious" to us. We casually count on their being true without thinking about them further.

But not a single one of these assumptions remains unchallenged by modern physics. Even time itself turns out to be a different experience for each observing mind. Descartes turned seventeenth-century thought upside down by saying that "I" am separate from the "world" and that I can therefore objectively experiment upon the world without having any mutually influential relationship *with* it. But quantum physics has shown that

Descartes was wrong. The very act of observing a phenomenon is part of the phenomenon. And every phenomenon I witness has simultaneous connections and repercussions throughout my entire being and throughout the entire universe.

Thus, science is converging on the much more traditional human standpoint that we are all part of a mutually interlaced world, that our conscious existence influences our environment (including each other) just as our environment influences us, and that our thoughts, feelings, and actions count, in the most total sense imaginable.

According to the evidence of our most advanced sciences, vibrations appear to be more fundamental than atoms or particles. Whereas the primary qualities of particles are their distinct separateness and inviolability, the primary qualities of vibrations are their universal interpermeability and interconnectedness. What this says about our world is shattering to the Newtonian point of view. Rather than living in a world built out of bits of isolated, mechanical matter, we live in a universe of unified, interweaving vibrations, in which each one of us is part of a vast dynamic harmony with everyone and everything else. This, the most esoteric idea of all, is being demonstrated by our new Western physics.

This newly reemerging worldview calls for a coincident healing art. The various investigations into vibrational healing may be the beginnings of this healing art. As Dr. George Vithoulkas writes, "if progress in such research continues as it seems to promise, we may well see the dawning of a new era in medicine – an era of *energy medicine*."[15]

TOWARD A COOPERATIVE DIVERSITY

The power of the medical establishment is rooted in the firm foundation that was built by the development of antibiotics and the subsequent subjugation of infectious disease. Today, this foundation is being challenged on three separate fronts. First, we now know that time and hygiene play at least as great a healing role as antibiotic therapy. Second, it is now more widely appreciated that the body's own resistance – as a function of heredity, stress, diet, environment, and the psyche – is at least as important as any infectious germ. Finally, the foundation itself is cracking under the strain of the *resurgence* of infectious disease. AIDS is not the only epidemic. Syphilis, tuberculosis, and many other such diseases are also currently on the rise. And they are returning with a vengeance. The process of drug-induced mutation has granted them new destructive powers while rendering them impervious to our strongest medicines. The age of infectious disease, we are learning to our dismay, is not over. It may prove to have hardly begun.

In her 1988 study of medicine and culture, Lynn Payer observes that overall mortality rates are quite similar in the United States, France, and England. Yet surgeries are performed twice as often here as in Great Britain. In fact, we perform three times as many mastectomies and six times as many coronary bypasses. *But our mortality rates end up no better.* Only 2.4 percent of all French women have had a hysterectomy, in contrast to the 2 percent of American women who undergo this treatment *every single year.* Drugs are used more extensively here than anywhere in Europe, and our prescribed dosages are almost uniformly higher. *But our mortality rates end up no better.* Payer notes that our overuse and abuse of medicine are symptoms of a forceful American need always to be "in control," plus a fear of malpractice. But mostly, as she suggests, it is due to a strangely distorted philosophical outlook that regards nature and our own human body as inept machines.[16]

This kind of thinking has got to change. We must take a fresh look at our approach to nature and to healing, and to the various healing arts and healing philosophies. Medicine, chiropractic, acupuncture, and homeopathy do not, of course, constitute the entire available range of healing arts. In addition to herbalism, osteopathy, and the esoteric therapies (such as the ones mentioned above) there are also dentistry, nursing, midwifery, nutrition, body work, and an endless array of other practices. My choice of subjects naturally reflects my own personal interests and knowledge, and is not intended either to be all-inclusive or to slight anyone. I have tried, however, within this limited discussion to raise a number of issues that are important in all the healing arts.

One such issue that needs further clarification is the issue of legitimate knowledge. For someone to say, for instance, that they believe in crystals does not necessarily mean that they know anything about crystals. To insist on believing in something that one actually knows nothing about, would seem a poor excuse for avoiding the effort required to find out the truth. I do not mean to imply that there is no possible knowledge regarding crystals: it is just that too many people are willing to "believe" in them and to stop at that. Unfortunately, this veil of unquestioning belief casts a pall of suspicion over anyone who might be genuinely engaged in an impartial study of the properties and capabilities of crystals, and may also keep a sick person from seeking necessary help of a more useful kind.

Certainly there may be a genuine tradition in which the use of crystals for healing has been studied and understood, and in which certain people have acquired the knowledge, wisdom, and skills necessary to use them effectively. It appears that such knowledge has been used by certain American Indian tribes, among others. But this does not mean that merely because someone wishes to do so that they thereby have this same ability. If it is true that crystals have remarkable healing powers, it seems unlikely that someone could learn how to use them just by attending a weekend seminar.

I do not mean to imply that knowledge can only be won through intellectual means. It can also be found through the emotions, it can be found through experience, it can be found through in-depth contemplation and meditation, and—at least for some people—it can be found intuitively. Nor by any means do I wish to imply that knowledge, to be "real" knowledge, must be in accord with our scientific point of view: Socrates and the Yellow Emperor both acquired unsurpassed amounts of knowledge and wisdom without the benefit of Newtonian materialism. But I do mean to imply that the acquisition of genuine knowledge always entails more than just wishing or assuming or believing. It requires effort. It requires payment. Ideas about the balance and harmony of nature should not be taken sentimentally. Nature can often be cruel. And acquiring an understanding of nature, be it the understanding of an Aristotle, a Lao-tzu, or an Einstein, takes great personal sacrifice and work.

I bring this all up because too often nonmedical approaches to healing and non-Newtonian approaches to life are belittled for the very good reason that the *presentation* of the approach is subjective, sentimental, or irrational in tone. This makes it difficult for us to see that the approaches themselves may, in fact, be quite objective, quite serious, and quite rational. And it makes it difficult for any useful dialogue to occur. But we are multidimensional beings living in a multidimensional, troubled world, and we need dialogue.

One issue that calls for dialogue is a very practical one. This "whole range of healing systems that the genius of the human race has so patiently worked out," as Ted Kaptchuk terms it, ought to be working together. We need a unified front of health practitioners, engaged in the friendly and impartial pursuit of what works best for our patients. Within the context of this harmonious effort, each healing art must retain its unique knowledge, its unique skills, and its unique point of view. But this very knowledge, these very skills, and all these diverse and fascinating points of view, could and should be fed into a magnificent cooperative venture.

No one healing art can be all things to all people. Different approaches are necessary for different people at different times. A cooperative effort, respectful of diversity and with the common aim of doing the most good for suffering humanity, must be the goal. I am suggesting, in fact, that we in the healing arts stop defending our particular beliefs and rather search together for what is objectively most true, and clinically most useful for our patients. This will not be easy, considering all the honest disagreement that will ensue as we jointly consider the best treatment for individual cases. And to be sure, we must avoid merely arriving at many separate evaluations and applying them to a single individual; a unifying philosophy is absolutely necessary to avoid confusion. It is my hope that the comprehensive theory of health and disease presented in the Introduction can help practitioners achieve this. Considered realistically, however, it is highly unlikely that the members of the various competitive healing arts will of themselves initiate such a change. It will only come about when forced upon us by a public that has grown tired of our unhealthful interprofessional squabbling.

4

Receptive Healing: Taking Good Care of Yourself

A receptive body is one that is strong, flexible, sensitive, resilient, expressive, poised, calm, and responsive. By acquiring such qualities, our bodies become suitable vehicles for love, work, and success. A body that is sustained by candy and chemicals, one that is weak and debilitated from lack of motion and fresh air and that is in a perpetual state of unconscious, rigid tension is unreceptive to healing and at least partially unresponsive to many of the joys and passions of life. We can help to turn this around by taking better care of ourselves, by means of good nutrition, exercise, breathing, movement, and relaxation.[1]

GOOD NUTRITION

After food is eaten, four processes must take place:

1. *Digestion.* First the food must be broken down into small particles that the body can make use of. Using mechanical churning, acid, and digestive enzymes (which break up food chemically), the digestive process occurs in the stomach and part of the small intestine.

2. *Absorption.* The tiny food particles must now pass through the permeable walls of the small intestine, where they are immediately picked up by the bloodstream for delivery to all parts of the body.

3. *Utilization.* The body must now be able to *use* the food

particles for growth, maintenance, repair, and energy production. This process naturally requires that our cells and organs be functioning in an appropriately healthy manner when the food arrives.

4. *Elimination.* Any undigested or indigestible foods—which will spoil and give off toxins—must be eliminated by the large intestine (also called the colon). Metabolic waste products and excesses found within the body must be eliminated by the kidneys.

Good nutrition must take into account all four processes. The choice of which foods to eat is only one part of the art of good nutrition. The importance of all four aspects can best be explained by taking an example:

Calcium is the most abundant mineral in the body. Ninety-nine percent of it is found in bones and teeth; the remaining one percent is dispersed in the blood and soft tissues (such as muscles and organs). Calcium is necessary for muscle contraction, blood clotting, a regulated heartbeat, nerve transmission, enzyme activity, bowel function, and sleep. Calcium itself, however, can only do its job in the presence of vitamin D, certain fatty acids, and certain hormones. Without enough acid in the gut, calcium cannot be properly digested (another reason for the value of the apple cider vinegar remedy). If the tissues are too alkaline, calcium will simply drop helplessly out of solution and possibly be deposited in joint spaces (where it can potentially cause arthritic problems), or it may fuse with cholesterol plaques in the blood vessels (thus contributing to hardening of the arteries).

Here two points are noteworthy. First, calcium is clearly needed for a whole variety of critical tasks. Second, a "problem" might not imply simply the need to eat more calcium. There might be a problem with stomach acid production, a deficiency in vitamin D or healthy dietary oils, or a problem with a hormone.

Now for the really bad news. Dairy products, in spite of all the Dairy Council's advertising to the contrary, are not a good source of calcium. It is true that milk is full of calcium, but little or none of that calcium can be absorbed by our intestines. Infants have particular enzymes for the digestion, absorption, and utilization of mother's milk. However, these enzymes either decrease or vanish altogether after weaning. Look at the animal kingdom: mammalian bodies are all extremely similar on the inside, but apart from humans and their pets, mammals do not drink milk after weaning. Cows produce gallons upon gallons of milk, rich with calcium, yet they themselves eat grass and grains – no cheese or yogurt or milk. Nature does put some enzymes and useful bacteria into the milk itself, in order to help the infant digest it; but pasteurization destroys these things. The milk we buy in the store is dead, inert, and useless, and thus may well be irritating to the lining of the intestines. In response to this irritation, the intestines protect themselves by producing extra mucus, which in turn can cause various unpleasant bowel symptoms. Also, because the body's "mucus response" is not limited to one area, the consumption of milk products often causes stuffy noses and clogged sinuses.

Before leaving the subject of bad sources of calcium, let's consider dolomite. Dolomite is rock. Rock is not food. You can save money on dolomite by going outside and eating the sidewalk. Sidewalks are full of calcium. So, by the way, are oyster shells. Neither are meant for human consumption.

But we do need calcium. Some possible symptoms of a calcium problem (which, as stated, might actually be a vitamin problem, an acid problem, a fat problem, or a hormone problem) might include arthritis pains, bursitis, stiffness, hives, itching, recurrent herpes outbreaks, severe menstrual pain, muscle cramps, or anxiety states. If a calcium supplement is really required, there are several forms: calcium orotate (the most utilizable but very expensive), calcium lactate (very utilizable and very cheap), calcium pantothenate, calcium gluconate, raw bone meal, etc. (I have deliberately left out antacids such as Tums, and I think it worth pointing out that no one has ever gotten osteoporosis because of a deficiency in Tums.) More important, there are other dietary sources of calcium besides milk. Calcium is found in abundance in most nuts and seeds, dried fruits, many vegetables (such as broccoli, spinach, turnips, and swiss chard), most beans (including soy beans, chickpeas, pinto beans, and azuki beans), most seafoods (such as sardines, oysters, trout, tuna, and swordfish), and for exotic tastes there are great stores of calcium in dandelion greens and seaweed. If you must consume dairy products, stick to yogurt, kefir, buttermilk, and the white cheeses, particularly goat cheeses. These highly-cultured products have had many useful enzymes and bacteria returned to them, and are therefore the least problematic.

You can see from the example of calcium that all four of the processes mentioned at the start of this chapter are important in nutrition. We are not simply "what we eat." It would be more correct to say that we are what we eat, digest, absorb, and utilize, all of which depends on a great many interrelated factors.

There is even more to it than that. Let's follow a few atoms of food on their journey through the human body. These tiny atoms are within a bit of food that first passes through the stomach, where the food is broken apart and mixed with water. Next, the atoms end up in the small intestines, where enzymes break down the food into its basic nutrients. Now absorbed into the bloodstream, these nutrients (including the atoms we are following) pass into the liver, where they are detoxified – that is, rid of any bacteria or poisons. The blood containing our atoms is now clean of poisons and rich with nutrients; however, it is very low in oxygen, which is utterly necessary if the body is going to be able to utilize these nutrients. So the atoms now flow with the bloodstream up to the heart and lungs, where the blood is revitalized with oxygen, pumped out of the heart, and sent off to feed the entire body (including the heart itself). Let's suppose our particular atoms flow up an artery into the brain. Some of these atoms are now absorbed into the brain tissue and are used in the production of chemicals that signal reactions in the hypothalamus (the "relay station" for thoughts and emotions, which I will discuss more fully in the next chapter). Some of the atoms now continue on as part of a newly produced hormone of the pituitary gland. Circulating again in the bloodstream, as hormones do, these atoms end up in the male testes or the female ovaries, where they will partake in the formation of sperm or the maturation of an egg.

Here again it is easy to see that we are not just what we eat. We are what we eat, breathe, think, and feel. And even this is tempered by our inheritance from parents and ancestors, depending on what *they* ate, breathed, thought, and felt: just as our children and their children will be affected by what *we* eat, breathe, think, and feel right now.

Carbohydrates

Carbohydrates consist of a string of "sugar molecules": the longer the chain, the more complex the carbohydrate. White flour, for instance, is a short-chain, "simple" carbohydrate (really just a few sugars). Whole grains are long-chain, "complex" carbohydrates. For purposes of blood sugar-level maintenance, the body is geared to digest, absorb, and utilize complex carbohydrates: white bread, white sugar, and the like, which our bodies are not naturally geared to deal with, are thus a stressful shock to the system.

Carbohydrates constitute our major source of available energy. That is, each of our cells is able to burn carbohydrates and to use the energy thus released to carry on its various functions.

Fats

Fats and oils, made of chains of "fatty acids," are also used for energy. But unlike carbohydrates, energy in this form can be stored for later use. In addition, fats and oils act as "carriers" for fat-soluble vitamins (that is, they aid such vitamins' absorption into the bloodstream), they provide cushioning and protection for vital organs, they are necessary structural elements of our cells, they are needed for the proper utilization of cholesterol and calcium, they are the substances out of which our cells make prostaglandins and many hormones, and they keep the skin and other tissues youthful and healthy looking. For all these reasons, even when one is dieting it is not a good idea to eliminate all fats and oils.

Protein

Protein, the body's building material, is made of various combinations of "amino acids." Our muscles, skin, organs, antibodies, and enzymes are all made of protein. The protein we eat is made of various amino acids that are connected together in very particular sequences (a different sequence for every type of protein). In digestion, we break this protein up into free, separate amino acids. Inside our cells, the amino acids are then rearranged and reconnected into new sequences, that is, new proteins. Our personal genetic DNA determines the particular order and sequence of amino acids in our personal proteins. In other words, our DNA determines what our protein, our body-building material, looks like. Speaking on this purely physical level, the kind of protein your DNA makes (depending on how your inherited DNA arranges your amino acids), is what makes you *you*.

Vitamins and Minerals

Vitamins and minerals are described in scientific terms as cofactors, or catalysts. That is, during the body's chemical processes (whereby various substances are broken down, built up, or burned for energy), vitamins and minerals are required to make the system work.

One role of vitamin C is to act as a catalyst in processes of tissue repair. It is important to note that if effective healing is not taking place because of a vitamin C deficiency, then taking vitamin C will help. But this does not necessarily imply that a person with an adequate supply of vitamin C will receive additional benefit from taking excess vitamin C. Such effects are still being debated, but in any case the possible benefits that an excess of a vitamin may have is not in its role as a vitamin! Vitamins are foods, and certain amounts are required by the body; but taking megadoses actually constitutes treating those vitamins like medical *drugs*, to see if sufficient quantities might have some artificial ability to change some process in the body. And this may prove to be the case! We may yet discover that megadoses of vitamins can help cure certain diseases. There is much important research currently going on in this field. But we do not know all the answers yet. In the meantime, since megadoses of vitamins, like any drug, can have unexpected and unwanted side effects, it is unwise to experiment on yourself.

Since vitamin C is water soluble, taking a little bit extra as a safeguard against deficiency (it is being used up constantly) is probably fine. Nutritional supplements do have value when used intelligently and sparingly. But it is not useful to take fifty pills a day. The body just gets overtaxed and confused. Our polluted environment may make some continuous supplementation advisable, but remember that supplements vary in quality, and people vary in needs at varying times. Before embarking on a regimen of pills, seek out responsible, professional guidance.

Chemists will often claim that the vitamins they synthesize in the laboratory are "just like" the vitamins in nature's foods. What they fail to remember is that vitamins in nature appear as intricately balanced complexes of *many* substances; we do not know what all these different substances are for, or what proportions and combinations are most effective, and we undoubtedly have not yet even found all the substances that are part of each total vitamin complex. If you get your vitamins from natural food sources, you know that you are getting everything you need in just the right combination, without having to depend on a chemist who might not know everything nature knows.

Water

Water makes up about two-thirds of our body weight. Digestion, absorption, utilization, elimination, and virtually every other bodily process – all require water. Indeed, the most important nutritional deficiency in the typical American diet today is water! The body is intelligent: it can tell the difference between water and other liquids. Orange juice has water in it, but you would not wash your floor with orange juice – it just doesn't work the same way. Your body is at least as discriminating as a kitchen floor. If you drink milk, juice, soda, coffee, and tea all day long, but no plain water, the body can easily become dehydrated. An average-sized adult should drink between five and eight glasses of pure water every day.

THE HEALTHY DIET

To be receptive to healing, the cells and tissues of our body must be sustained by a healthy, wholesome diet. But there is a point about moderation that needs to be made here, and I cannot say it better than Snoopy:

Reprinted by permission of UFS, Inc.

When great stress is building up, we may need to indulge a physical impulse as well as an emotional one. It is better to have a cigarette, or a hot fudge sundae, than to shoot heroin or go on a violent rampage. Balance is the point, not fanaticism. Fanatical overdiscipline is a terrible stress. A little vice is better than a big perversion. Sometimes committing a little vice is the safest, most responsible thing we can do.

Think of it this way. There is a wolf inside us, and there is a lamb. These are integral parts of our personalities. The lamb is innocent, happy, kind, and playful. The wolf is none of these. He is mean, selfish, self-indulgent, and none too friendly. If he gets too hungry, if his needs are never satisfied, he is going to eat the lamb! It is terribly dangerous to ignore him, to starve him, to anger him by pretending that he is unimportant, too contemptible for our consideration, or not really there. Like it or not, he is always there.

Besides, he might come in handy some day. If you are ever in great danger, you cannot count on a lamb for much. It is better to have a friendly wolf on your side. Don't forget to feed the wolf.

The moderate, healthful diet will include all – or almost all – of the following categories:

Grains and Cereals

Rather than center the diet on meats, center it on nuts, seeds, grains, and beans. These foods can provide all the protein we need, the healthiest oils, and the finest complex carbohydrates.

Fruits and Vegetables

Fruits and vegetables are, of course, excellent foods. Arthritics should avoid citrus fruits, however, and anyone with a sugar-handling problem should stay away from overripe or excessively sweet fruits.

Vegetables are best served raw, steamed, or sautéed briefly in olive oil. (When an oil gets hot, it changes chemically into a harmful substance. Olive oil, however, has to reach a temperature much higher than the usual cooking temperatures before this happens. Since olive oil is also an extremely valuable nutrient to begin with, it is clearly the best choice for cooking.)

Dairy Products

If you enjoy milk, try to drink raw, farm-fresh milk or goat's milk, and only drink it occasionally.

Butter is food. Margarine, which is made from chemicals and hydrogenated oil (no matter what kind of oil it started with), is *not* food. Do not use margarine. Instead, try the following recipe for a healthy heart:

> *Missy's Better Butter*
>
> Mix in a blender:
> 1 cup safflower oil
> 1/2 lb (2 sticks) butter
> 2 tablespoons water

> 1 teaspoon lecithin (available in health
> food stores and pharmacies)

Refrigerate and use just like butter.

Let me insert here a word about cholesterol. Cholesterol has been found to build up in the form of plaques on the inner lining of arteries, thus increasing blood pressure and inducing life-threatening clots. Autopsy studies from the Korean and Vietnam wars have demonstrated that this serious condition is a major problem even for most twenty-year-old Americans.

The most popular approach to this problem is the reduction of cholesterol in the diet. It is an unrealistic effort, however, since only about 20 percent of the cholesterol in our bodies comes from the food we eat. The rest is made by the liver, and if we eat less cholesterol, the liver simply makes more.

There is a good reason for the body's maintenance of its cholesterol production. Brain tissue is full of cholesterol, many hormones are made from it, it lubricates the blood vessels and is a structural element in all our cells. Cholesterol problems can usually be resolved not by trying to eliminate this valuable substance, but by getting the body to utilize it properly. Why, for so many Americans, is that not occurring naturally today?

In order to use cholesterol, the body needs three factors:

1. Unsaturated vegetable oils—the same ones the body needs to make anticlotting, anti-inflammatory prostaglandins: safflower oil, sesame oil, linseed oil, olive oil, and so on.
2. Various B vitamins, particularly choline, inositol (which together make up lecithin), and niacin.
3. Oxygen from aerobic exercise.

Instead of our having these elements readily available in our bodies, too often here is what happens:

1. Our diets are full of heavily saturated animal fats, with not nearly enough raw, unsaturated vegetable oil.
2. We refine out all the vitamin B from our foods (Incidentally, eggs and butter are full of lecithin).

3. Finally, we get insufficient or inappropriate exercise.

Thus we turn a life-giving substance like cholesterol into a killer, and then we blame the cholesterol. Genetic enzyme problems and other serious medical pathologies can, of course, be the cause of certain types of cholesterol excess, and blood-pressure medications or low-cholesterol diets are sometimes necessary. But these problems account for only a relatively few of the most severe cases. The massive epidemic of clogged arteries in our society is due to poorly handled stress, pollution, and poor nutrition. And we endanger ourselves by believing that so long as we cut down on eggs and take our medication, we can go on eating diets high in animal fats and refined carbohydrates and can continue to lead sedentary lives.

Meats

Meats contain both value and danger, and should be eaten in moderation. Avoid fatty meats, salt-cured meats, charcoal-broiled meats, and processed meats containing nitrates (bologna, bacon, hot dogs, etc.). There is much disagreement in health food circles about the benefits of vegetarianism, and the discussions often border on nothing more than righteous indignation and moral fanaticism. As you make your own decision about consuming meat, consider the following points:

• We do not need meat to get enough protein and to be physically healthy.
• Our diets tend to be poisonously overloaded with animal fats, causing problems with prostaglandin balance and cholesterol utilization.
• The amount of landspace used to feed cattle could be used to grow enough grain to feed many more hungry people.
• A synchrony exists (which I will discuss further in chapter 5) between emotions and body chemistry. The grotesquely inhumane treatment of commercial feed animals breeds pain, stress, frustration, and terror. The meat we eat is filled with the literal chemical results of this.

- Moreover, feed animals are raised on diets of synthetic hormones, growth stimulants, antibiotics, and other poisonous drugs. These, too, leave residues in our meat. (Animal blood transmits animal *Ch'i*, the chemical results of their emotions, and the poisons of their diets. This may be part of the reason for the traditional kosher custom of draining meat of all blood).

- In order to replenish grazing land for cattle, forested areas twice the size of Denmark are destroyed every year! This huge loss of green forests dramatically changes the atmosphere's ability to handle water, oxygen, and carbon dioxide, and leads to massive droughts and a worsening of the "greenhouse effect."

- High-meat diets have been clearly linked to cancer, heart disease, osteoporosis, and other illnesses. Vegetarians who contract cancer have much better survival statistics than meateaters.

- Nonetheless, whereas a body that has evolved in Tahiti or Japan may fare well on one type of diet, a body whose ancestors came from eastern Europe or Sweden may require a different diet. People of European stock who live in temperate climates may do better with some meat in their diets.

- A strictly vegetarian diet may be useful for a life of contemplation and meditation, but having some animal food in the diet may be necessary for most active participants in today's stressful Western world.

- Plants are alive too. We have to eat something! The world is built on a system of life consuming life. The Buddha is reported to have said, "It is not the eating of meat that renders one impure, but being brutal, hard, pitiless, miserly."

If you choose to eat meat, eat it rare, since rare meat appears to have some healing value for the adrenal glands. Well-done meat is difficult to digest and thus remains a very long time in the intestinal tract, where it may even spoil—creating gas, indigestion, and possibly carcinogens. As always, look to nature: carnivores do not overcook their meat.

Beverages

Drink primarily water! Fruit and vegetable juices are also healthful (so long as they are not fruit "drinks," full of sugar and preservatives). However, pasteurization and modern bottling procedures neutralize many of the beneficial elements in juices, so it is worthwhile to buy a juicer and make one's own. Other useful beverages include herbal teas and occasional small quantities of cultured dairy drinks.

Sweeteners

Honey, molasses, and pure maple syrup are somewhat better for the system than white sugar. Use these in moderate quantities. A sweet tooth can often be satisfied with fresh or dried fruit, apple butter, peanut butter, and so on.

Snacks

Seeds, nuts, high-quality nut butters, moderate amounts of cheese (not "cheese foods"), rice cakes, plain yogurt, and of course fresh vegetables, fresh fruit, and dried fruit are all appropriate snack items.

Most people are tired of being bombarded with the contradictory information we receive every day from books, newspapers, and talk shows. So now that we have discussed so many details, I am going to cut through all the confusion and simplify the entire science of nutrition down to one simple rule. I guarantee that if you will struggle to follow this one simple rule, it will eliminate most dietary problems. Here, then, is the only real "rule" of nutrition:

When you eat, eat food.

That is really all there is to it. If you read a label and your intuition tells you "this doesn't sound like food," don't eat it. If it is a color you have never seen in nature, don't eat it. That will take care of 99 percent of all dietary problems. To take care of the rest:

1. Relax
2. Become knowledgeable
3. Pay attention to your own body

If we can follow these simple principles, our bodies will not be nearly so receptive to disease.

ELIMINATION

In relation to our overall nutrition, we still need to consider one more bodily process. The body must constantly rid itself of waste. The large intestine eliminates feces; the skin, sweat; the kidneys, urine; and the lungs, exhaled air. All three forms of matter (solid, liquid, gas) are thus filtered out and cleansed perpetually and the wastes removed. If any of these functions are interrupted, self-poisoning will occur, causing illness and eventually death.

The Colon

The bacteria in the colon (called "intestinal flora") form vitamin K – a vitamin essential for blood to clot, and one that is not usually found in sufficient quantities in food. Several B vitamins, including B-12, are also given to us by these bacteria. These "good" bacteria also help to break down waste products, for ease of removal.

Other bacteria produce gas. These latter, "bad" bacteria prefer an alkaline environment, which means that excessive bowel gas is another symptom of too little acid.

Different kinds of diets will encourage the proliferation of different intestinal bacteria. For instance, two particular species of bacteria flourish in the colons of people on a typical, modern, low-roughage, refined diet. These bacteria are known to convert some of the bile that reaches the colon into carcinogens. In contrast to these, other, useful bacteria are predominant in people on a diet of healthy, whole foods (including generous quantities of fiber).

It should be noted that fiber is a natural part of food, as are the vitamins, minerals, complex carbohydrates, complete proteins, and healthy fats and oils that we all need. The synthetic fiber substitutes that manufacturers put into supermarket items (after refining out everything of nutritional value) do *not* fulfill the body's requirements for healthy fiber. To get fiber, we must eat whole grains and fresh, raw vegetables.

A low-fiber diet, coupled with stress and a deficiency in water, leads to the result that millions of Americans suffer some kind of bowel problem. Bowel movements should occur once or twice each day. They should not be uncomfortable. The stool should be brown (not yellow or gray). There should be no signs of undigested foods, mucus, or blood. The stool should be long, thick, and well-formed, rather than small, narrow, or hard. It should not be necessary to read half the daily newspaper while waiting. It should not require a cigarette and a cup of coffee in order to "get moving." The stool should not have a strong, offensive odor. Any of these signs indicates a colon problem that should be dealt with before it turns into something more serious. They are a signal that feces are not being properly eliminated from the body, but are building up in the body and literally spoiling. The result can be

- Irritation and inflammation in the colon
- Absorption of poisonous substances into the bloodstream
- Deficiencies in vitamin K, vitamin B-12, and potassium
- Dangerous imbalances in the intestinal flora, which may lead to yeast infections or other serious problems

It may be useful to periodically cleanse the colon more quickly than can be accomplished by simply improving the diet. Various intestinal cleansing products are sold in health food stores. Generally, these contain a clay substance called bentonite (which helps to clean the lining of the small intestine) along with ground psyllium seeds (an herb that helps to clean out the large intestine). Other healing herbs may be included. These substances, plus a good deal of water, a much improved diet, and some exercise will have a highly beneficial effect on the entire intestinal tract, and can often eliminate all the symptoms that may be related to poor functioning. In addition, the occasional use of enemas or a colonic irrigation (a painless colonic "washing," usually administered by a trained colonic therapist, although there are home colonic units available) can be of immense value in cleaning out putrefied material. Various other natural therapies may also improve intestinal function.

Finally, it must be noted that sitting is not the appropriate position of defecating. The shape and position of the colon, as well as those of the surrounding muscles and organs, require a natural squatting position in order to function efficiently in maintaining internal cleanliness. Returning to this normal bowel habit would in itself prevent a great many bowel problems.

Good food is of no value without good elimination and all the other factors. We are what we eat, breathe, absorb, think, and feel, what we do, and (unfortunately) what we fail to eliminate.

The Kidneys and the Skin

The kidneys' job is to clean the blood of metabolic wastes and excesses and to eliminate these by passing them out in urine. The first consideration for all kidney problems is water. Without enough clean, pure water, the kidneys may become congested with poisons. If these poisons are not continuously flushed out with water, the kidneys cannot keep up with their task of filtering the blood.

This can result in the following problems:

• Toxins back up in the blood, causing self-poisoning.
• Swelling may occur in different parts of the body. When only a small amount of water is available in the body, the body tends to hold on to it in order to dilute any toxic wastes that concentrate in the tissues. Paradoxical though it sounds, the best way to get rid of most swelling is to drink more water.
• If the urine itself is not dilute enough, mineral wastes may accrete and form kidney or bladder stones.
• Skin irritations may develop. Sweating is another means by which we filter and cleanse liquids in the body. If the kidneys are unable to work at their best, the skin may pitch in to help, and excessive amounts of toxins will pass through the pores. In other words, many skin problems can be improved or eradicated by just drinking more water!

An extremely healthful practice that supports the process of elimination is the steam bath. A good, long steam bath will produce several effects in addition to soothing tired muscles:

1. It will open up the skin's pores and cause profuse sweating. The chemical composition of sweat is almost identical to the composition of urine; thus sweating is an excellent way to help clean and detoxify the body. (You also lose a lot of water in a steam bath, though, so be sure to drink an extra glass of water that day.)
2. It will artificially cause a brief, slight fever, which may help to prevent problems with latent bacteria and viruses.
3. It will stimulate the general metabolism, speeding up the various bodily processes and stimulating the immune system.

When taking a steam bath, splash yourself occasionally with cold water. This increases the above-mentioned benefits, and it also has value in stimulating the adrenal glands. A twenty-minute steam bath (*not* a dry sauna) several times a week is healthy, invigorating, and rejuvenating.

FASTING

One important way to help keep the body receptive to healing is by fasting. Fasting does not do anything in an "active" sense; rather, it is a period of physiological rest that allows the body to cleanse and heal.

There is a great difference between fasting and starving. The body must continually use the nutrients we have eaten, so that it is able to produce energy and to carry on its various necessary metabolic functions. If we temporarily stop eating new food, the body has a several-days' reserve of food in the small intestines. Once this source is gone, the body has a many-days' reserve of food held in the fatty tissues and other tissues (such as the liver) that store nutrients. Finally, when this too is gone, the body will burn up all the internal accumulations of toxins that tend to get stored throughout the tissues, especially in our polluted times.

Up to this point, the body has actually been getting rid of unnecessary fat and poison. And during this tremendously useful process, which generally takes about six weeks to complete, all the digestive and absorptive functions of the body are at rest. This process is called *fasting*.

Ultimately, when the intestinal food, excess fat, and toxic waste deposits are all used up, we must begin eating again. Otherwise the body will be forced to burn up and metabolize its own useful structural tissue (that is, the muscles and organs themselves). This is called *starving.*

You can die of starvation. You cannot die of fasting. Nonetheless, many things can happen during a fast, and no one should ever go on a fast for more than a few days without supervision. Also, you must not stop drinking water. On the contrary, since the body is detoxifying on a fast, you need plenty of extra water to keep flushing the kidneys clean.

It is not a good idea to fast when under severe stress, because the fast itself could then become an additional stress. Since a fast is a time of physiological rest, it should be conducted under restful, quiet, warm conditions, with professional supervision.

This does not mean, however, that the faster is confined to bed, weeping with dire sensations of painful hunger. Quite the contrary: after the first few days, the purely psychological habit of being constantly "hungry" goes away. Most fasters then feel more energized, more clearheaded, and more alive than ever. There may be some difficult periods when the body's detoxification causes discomfort (which is why supervision is necessary), but most fasters report that a properly conducted fast feels great.

A total fast means that you subsist on water only. Other, easier procedures are also of much value, and may often be very effective for the average person who cannot spend six weeks fasting at a professionally staffed retreat. I spoke earlier of the intestinal cleansers, bentonite and psyllium seeds. The ground-up seeds tend to expand in the stomach, giving a feeling of fullness. A week-long semifast consisting of these products, lots of fresh vegetable juices and fruit juices, plenty of spring water, and several enemas or colonics, is an easy, comfortable, and extremely beneficial procedure. It may be best to adapt your body to this by conducting a three-day semifast each month, or a one-day semifast each week, and then—when it feels right—following the procedure for a full week. Most people find such a week to be surprisingly easy. It is healthy, restful, and cleansing, and will improve digestion, absorption, utilization, and elimination. It is an excellent annual or biannual habit.

Mankind has safely employed fasting throughout history to enhance the receptive force of healing. Animals and young children know instinctively that when they are sick they must rest and stop eating. A day or two without food will not kill anyone; on the contrary, it increases energy and recuperative powers by making us more receptive. The notion that we can "keep our strength up" only by constantly eating is an illusion: indeed, we often eat ourselves into early graves. Keep in mind that the processes of absorption, utilization, and elimination are equally as important as digestion itself, and you will see that fasting is a part of healthy nutrition and healthy living. The value of the fasting period as a time to cleanse our bodies, to rest, and to reflect cannot be overstated.

EXERCISE

Physical exercise is a necessary means for relieving stress. Exercise purposefully redirects the nervous tension of the "fight or flight" response, stimulates the immune system and other internal systems, helps us sweat out toxins, and clears the head of negativity. People who regularly exercise have fewer illnesses than those who do not. In fact, here's one piece of information worth considering: research conducted in 1960 revealed that injected extracts of exercised muscle slowed the growth of cancerous tumors in mice and sometimes completely eliminated them, whereas injected extracts of nonexercised muscle had no effect. Exercise can make one look and feel great. It increases strength, prevents obesity, strengthens the heart and lungs—and it is fun.

That's when exercise is done right.

When done wrong, exercise can lead to fatigue, irritability, and depression, it can encourage us to "binge out" on fattening foods, can leave the body filled with extra poisons, and leads to sprained ankles and wrenched backs.

Since most of us no longer live a physical life-style in the great outdoors, regular exercise has become a natural, necessary part of healthy living. But different types of exercise have different effects, and certain physical principles must be understood in order to make exercise a benefit and not a problem. There is a great difference between "fitness" and "health." Too many people are becoming more "fit" and yet more "unhealthy." Fitness is the ability of the muscles to do work. As a side benefit of fitness, we look more trim and sexy. And since the heart is itself a muscle, a stronger heart is also one of the results. Health, a much broader concept, is a state of optimum well-being in which every cell, fiber, organ, system, thought, and emotion is working perfectly. Fitness should be *part* of health. Improper exercise, however, can *ruin* your health.

The most important thing to understand about exercise is the difference between aerobics and anaerobics.

Aerobic Muscle Fibers

---

1. Aerobic fibers are for long, steady, *endurance* work.
2. Aerobic fibers burn *fat* for energy.
3. To do this, they require *oxygen*. The oxygen is carried in the muscle by molecules of *iron*.

Anaerobic Muscle Fibers

---

1. Anaerobic fibers are for brief, powerful *spurts* of work.
2. Anaerobic fibers burn *sugar* for energy.
3. They do not require any oxygen, but this burning process does require *vitamin* B.

Both types of fibers are certainly necessary, and it is advantageous to exercise both. But most exercise should be aerobic, so let's talk about why that is so, and how to do it right.

The problem with a lot of today's exercise is simply that people tend to exercise at a low level of efficiency and a high level of stress. Rapid aerobic classes with constant admonitions to work harder and "make it burn" are actually *an*aerobic classes. Sprinting, lifting a heavy weight with one powerful thrust, and other examples of fast, exhausting work, all use anaerobic fibers. This means that you are burning sugar, which quickly lowers your blood sugar level. When this happens too often the adrenal glands become overly stressed and you begin to feel all those symptoms of "hypoglycemia"—tiredness, irritability, sleeplessness, fatigue, nervousness, depression, and hunger! Why bother? You feel lousy, and if one of your aims is to lose weight this is the last way you want to feel! Furthermore, anaerobic activity requires vitamin B. Because we tend to be deficient in vitamin B (refined foods like white bread and white rice remove the natural vitamin B, and then "enrich" it with heaven knows what), and since we lose whatever vitamin B we still have by sweating (B is water soluble), our anaerobic fibers are forced to work inefficiently and injuries are often the consequence. Finally, without enough vitamin B our bodies are unable to utilize cholesterol properly; the result is that cholesterol gets packed away in the arteries, thus negating any good effects the exercise may have had on your heart. In short, excessive anaerobic exercise increases stress, leads to obesity, injuries, and fatigue, and is bad for the heart.

If you wish to lose weight you must burn fat, not sugar. If you wish to have a healthy cardiovascular system, you must have plenty of oxygen in your tissues and plenty of vitamin B from whole foods. By exercising mostly aerobically rather than anaerobically, you accomplish all of the above while avoiding the problems associated with low blood sugar. In fact, aerobic exercise energizes us, clears the head, and suppresses hunger! This makes exercise worthwhile.

To function efficiently, aerobic fibers need iron. Iron deficiency can thus be another ultimate cause of injuries. Furthermore, without enough iron, there will be inefficient burning of fat—which means that if you are trying to lose weight you must have adequate iron in your system. Since women have a constant tendency to be deficient in iron, due to its loss each month in menstrual blood, this can often be a reason why a woman gets no satisfactory results from exercise and gives up. It is possible to be deficient in iron in the muscles but still have enough in your blood that a blood test fails to show anemia. If you think this might apply to you, and you wish to take an iron supplement, choose one that is "chelated" and comes from food sources that are natural to the body. Many iron pills are about as useful as chewing on your car. And only take a low dose – thirty milligrams or less per day – to avoid constipation.

Now let's discuss exactly what it means to exercise aerobically. I have said that aerobic muscle fibers are for steady endurance activity rather than for quick bursts of force. To be sure that you are using your aerobic fibers, you must not drive your body above a certain pace or effort. What we need is a way to determine what that pace ought to be, and a way to measure our pace while exercising so that we can keep to the proper level of effort. The simplest way of gauging the pace and effort your body is exerting is to monitor the rate at which your heart (a muscle) is beating. If your heart is beating too slowly, you are merely doing nothing effective. If it beats too rapidly, you have switched into anaerobic activity.

Therefore, to be exercising aerobically, the heart must be beating within a certain range – the "aerobic range" – and you want always to keep your heart rate *within that range* during exercise. Unfortunately, there is no perfect method for determining one's ideal range; different experts offer different formulas. Still, they all come out within a few points of one another. Here, then, is a simple formula for determining your aerobic heart-rate range:

1. Subtract your age from the number 220 (e.g., if you are thirty-five years old, $220 - 35 = 185$).
2. Then take 80 percent of that number (e.g., $185 \times .80 = 148$).
3. This number is the top of your range. To find the bottom, just subtract ten points (e.g., if you are thirty-five years old, your aerobic range is from 138 to 148 heartbeats per minute.)

While you are exercising, you want to work hard enough to keep your heart beating at a rate of at least 138 beats each minute (in our example for the thirty-five-year-old), but not so hard as to allow it to beat faster than 148 times per minute. As long as you stay within this ten-point range, you are exercising the right way: aerobically. If you wish to be healthy (not merely fit, which might even imply unhealthy), then you must perform 80 to 95 percent of your exercise within your aerobic range.

If you start out in terrible shape, walking around the block may be more than enough exercise to get your heart beating in your aerobic range! If so, then walking around the block is all you must do! When you are in better shape, because your body and heart are much stronger, you will find that you can now play a game of racquetball without pushing your heart beyond its aerobic range. You see, "aerobics" has nothing to do with the particular sport or exercise. Running can be aerobic or anaerobic, weight lifting can be aerobic or anaerobic, an exercise class can be aerobic for you and anaerobic for the person next to you; it only depends upon how fast *your* heart is beating. With patience, your strength and stamina will increase, your body will look and feel good, and your heart will become strong and healthy. Thus, even though your range will not change (until next year, and then only slightly), the kind of exercise and sports you can enjoy will change.

As you may have realized, the actual method for measuring the heart rate while exercising presents a bit of a problem. The simplest approach is to stop for a moment and take your pulse. But if you are in reasonably good shape, your heart rate will tend to slow down by about 1.5 beats per second when you stop exercising. (In fact, if you stop exercising and your heart does not quickly slow down, this is a sure sign that you are in very bad shape and are overdoing it). Therefore, by the time you stop, locate your pulse, look at your watch, count beats for fifteen seconds, and multiply by four, the answer you get can be 20 points lower than the actual "while exercising" count. Remember, your whole range is only 10 points. If you accept this number, you will assume that you are not working hard enough.

But chances are if you then pick up the pace, you will actually be shifting into *an*aerobic activity. Checking your pulse, therefore, is not a very reliable method.

The most reliable method is to buy an electronic device, available in many sporting goods stores, which consists of a simple strap around the chest that continuously monitors your heart rate while you exercise. A watchband may give you a reading at a glance, or the device may "beep" when you are out of range.

If you are training for a competitive sport, or are just heavily involved in an exercise program because you love it, then I strongly advise you to buy one of these devices. For the rest of us, there is another way to approach this. Before discussing that, though, let's look at a few more principles of healthy exercise.

1. To really do your body some good and really make some changes, you have to exercise at least four times each week (five or six times is better). Once you are in the condition you want, three times a week should maintain it: but to get there, a minimum of four. (As you get past the age of forty, it is best not to do the very same exercise two days in a row. Do different things, to prevent excessive wear and tear with insufficient time for tissue recovery.)

2. Part of the definition of *aerobic* is that it is steady and continuous. Therefore, to get results you must exercise in your range for a minimum of fifteen minutes per day. This must be at one time, not five minutes in the morning, ten in the afternoon. Eventually try to build up to one hour.

3. It is important not to alternate back and forth between aerobic exercise and anaerobic exercise. *You* can slow down right away from a quick sprint, but your body's chemistry cannot. Stay within range.

4. Warming up is important for several reasons. It takes a few minutes of a steady warm-up to get all of a muscle's aerobic fibers "turned on" and working. You also need some warm-up time to get blood into the muscles, which provides heat, nutrients, oxygen, and the ability to carry off waste products. If you jump into activity too quickly, before all the fibers are working and before all the supplies have arrived, the resulting inefficiency will lead to injuries.

5. If you do not take some time to steadily "cool down" after exercise, it will not affect your *fitness* one way or the other. But *neglecting to cool down is one of the worst things you can ever do to your health.* During exercise, your blood circulation shifts the greater part of its volume to the muscles. As exercise continues, metabolic wastes are poured into this blood—a normal event in physiology. If you just suddenly stop, this toxin-ridden blood is quickly shifted back to your internal organs. In particular, the kidneys must now filter out this waste. If this happens too quickly, the kidneys become congested and you become toxic and fatigued. Because of this toxicity, exercise can ruin your health if you habitually neglect a cool-down. You should take a good third as much time cooling down as you spent exercising in range. (Using running as an example, "cool down" means that you slow your pace steadily downward, first to a trot, then a fast walk, and finally a slow walk.)

6. Running is an excellent activity, involving an easy "spring" and a relaxed upper body. Jogging, with all that clunking around, is a terrible activity. If you have any tendency to incur injury, this will do it. Joggers are what make chiropractors like me get rich. It is best to find a running expert who can teach you to run the right way. High-impact aerobic classes create many of the same problems as jogging, which is why low-impact classes are becoming more popular.

Finally we come to the simplest way to measure whether you are correctly exercising within your aerobic range or not: if exercise leaves you fatigued, irritable, unhappy about your results, emotionally depressed, sick, fat, hungry, and injured, then you are not exercising in your range! This is good news! It means that the only real "rule" of exercise is this:

When you exercise, have fun.

Nature's rules aren't really so bad.

BREATHING, MOVEMENT, AND RELAXATION

One of the most difficult things for any of us to do is to relax. Our musculature is in a constant state of tension, even when we are asleep. This sustained tension is worth considerable emphasis, because it leads to so many unwanted results. It leads to fatigue, exhaustion, stiffness, and pain; it leads to headaches, insomnia, and stomachaches; it makes us clumsy, uncoordinated, accident-prone, and unattractive; it prevents us from recognizing important signals that our body may be giving us in the form of subtle sensations. Tension prevents us from taking in sufficient oxygen and from expelling carbon dioxide; it cuts us off from physical sensations of pleasure, and may even precipitate impotence and frigidity; it separates us from our emotions, dulls our thinking, weakens our will, and makes us unresponsive to the needs and existence of those around us; it blocks the free circulation of nerve energy, blood, and *ch'i*; it causes our bodies to deteriorate and age more quickly; and it leaves us helplessly unreceptive to healing, or any other divine force. To feel something deeply, to express oneself clearly, to understand anything completely – all of this requires a relaxed body. But we become dull and lifeless when our breathing muscles form a habit of only allowing short gasps of air, and never exhaling completely; when our pelvic muscles are tightly locked, blocking all the psychic and emotional energy of sexuality; when our neck, face, shoulder, and back muscles are rigid and painful; when, in short, we forget to relax, breathe, sense ourselves, and appreciate our physical existence.

Why are we the victims of so much chronic tension? There are many reasons. Most of us have ancient tapes in our heads that still command us to "stand up straight, hold that stomach in, and wipe that smile off your face!" Each time a child resists the normal impulse to cry, yell, laugh, or run, muscles learn to retract and to hold on to tension. Physical pains from bruises or sickness cause nearby muscles to tightly "guard" us, and this mechanism often slips into our unconsciousness and becomes a chronic habit. Early on, we discover that our deepest emotions are associated physically with deep breathing; in order to protect ourselves from emotional pain, we pull our upper body muscles in so that they become small and tight, leading to shallow breathing, dulled emotions, and small, tight lives. Fearful, puzzled, or embarrassed by sexuality, our leg muscles and pelvic muscles lock into safe positions. We are taught to think of our body as something separate from ourselves, often an encumbrance, made up of isolated parts—each of which must be entrusted to a specific specialist in order to keep it from hurting us. As we sink deeper into this fragmented materialist viewpoint, the body becomes less alive, less animated, and less important ("just a machine")—until it finally tightens up out of sheer neglect. And of course being relaxed, letting our lungs empty, and making ourselves receptive implies vulnerability, loss of control, and surrender. Everything in our personality seems to cringe at the mere thought of this.

A good habit for starting each day is mentally to go through the different sections of the body, sensing all the different tensions, and then gently, deliberately, relaxing them one at a time. Do not try to relax before you have quietly noticed where you are tense: you cannot correct a problem you do not know you have! You will most likely find that the pelvic and jaw muscles are habitually tense, and then you will likely discover that the muscles in your back, the back of your neck, and the backs of your legs, are tighter than the muscles in the front. In response to this, the looser muscles in front tend to droop, causing big bellies and stooped shoulders. But you can see that the way to correct this problem is not to "hold your stomach in" or "force your shoulders back," but rather to relax! When the back muscles relax, the belly and shoulders will simply sink into place. When you have relaxed your entire body, notice your breathing. Breathing should be slow and steady into the belly, exhalation should be complete, and there should be a slight pause before inhaling. But this is not a set of rules to memorize and follow. This is the normal instinctive pattern of breathing that a relaxed body will allow you to rediscover: rather than *learning* how to breathe, we need to *remember* how to breathe, to rediscover individually our own unique patterns and timing. Over time, they can become second nature, without any active effort.

After you have spent a few moments relaxing your way mentally through the body, take some time to experiment with all the different bodily movements which are possible. Let your body go, gently, without straining, and try to take up all the space you can. Try to stay completely relaxed and to use only those muscles necessary for each particular movement, imagining that you are bringing light and life back into each muscle, and that you are expressing yourself totally and joyously, the way children do. (Children don't need to exercise, because they know how to play. We too can learn once again how to play, and this is definitely an essential part of the healing process.) See if you can get every part of your body moving at once, including all the fingers, toes, hips, and nose. Try moving faster than you have ever moved before. Try moving slower than you have ever moved before. Try to find movements your limbs and torso have never done before. Enjoy knowing that you most definitely do look silly, never strain yourself, and remember to have fun: in fact, if at all possible, laugh. The body loves to move, though in our heads we may have forgotten this simple truth. Remember, also, to breathe, slowly and deeply into the belly, and particularly remember to exhale as much air as you inhale. Let it out with a deep, roaring, moan. Feel how your body vibrates with the sound.

Then, throughout the day, whenever you think of it, mentally look your body over and notice how many muscles are working that have nothing at all to do with what you are doing! If you are sitting at a desk writing, the calf muscles and jaw muscles do not have to be contracted; notice them, tighten them up even more for a brief instant, and then let them go. If you are cleaning the kitchen, the pelvic muscles and eye muscles do not need to be tense. Because we are constantly wasting our energy by over-working muscles that are totally unnecessary to the particular task at hand, we often find ourselves fatigued and exhausted by midafternoon even though we may have hardly "done" anything. Relaxation does not mean sitting around being lazy. Relaxation means only using those muscles that are necessary for what we are doing in a given moment, be it watching TV or carrying a refrigerator up a flight of stairs. The trick is not to become "lazy," but to learn how to relax and be active at the same time. If we can learn to do this, then productive, efficient, relaxed work will actually *increase* our energy, rather than make us tired.

As adults, most of us are faced with the necessity of having to relearn how to breathe, move, and relax. This act of remembrance requires time, effort, and probably some skilled help. Learning techniques of body awareness is a necessary part of healthy living. There are many fine systems of "body work" available: the Alexander Technique helps us remember how to sit, stand, walk, and move according to principles of relaxation, openness, and efficiency; massage aids us in relaxing the musculature, relieving tensions, and relieving stress; Body/Mind Centering helps to get us back in touch with essential sensations, reflexes, and movement patterns that we have lost over the years; psychological theater exercises can teach us to use the body as a fine instrument for expressing ideas, and for moving with ease, confidence, and grace; *t'ai chi,* the ancient Chinese martial art system that is also part of Chinese medicine, is actually a moving meditation for putting us in touch with, and in control of, our inner force and vitality; Rolfing and deep muscle massage break up fixations and help return our bodies to a state of suppleness and resilience; Feldenkrais work, Trager work, Hatha yoga, Shiatsu, and other methods too numerous to mention can all be of great value in helping us to return our bodies to a relaxed, open, receptive state.

Professionals in these areas, along with trainers, coaches, aerobics instructors, and nutritionists can all play important roles in our work to become and remain healthy by taking good care of ourselves.

Healing requires a mysterious intermingling of responsible action with utter passivity. It requires that we seek safe, active ways to stimulate, support, and encourage the body's healing activities. It requires that we treat ourselves well, with good food, exercise, movement, breathing, and, most important, relaxation. As we shall see in the next chapter, it also requires that we keep our mind, emotions, and spirit turned in the direction of health, wholeness, and love.

And at the same time, the process of healing also requires that we do nothing. All of the above activities are designed to enhance the forces of healing, but we also need simply to get out of the way. The most important way of enhancing the receptive force of healing, which *must* take place if we are to heal, is to find a stillness in the heart, mind, and body. Before healing can come to us, we have to surrender to healing. And before surrender can take place, there must be acceptance. We first have to accept what fate has brought us, with no judgment and no animosity. Only with complete acceptance of our fate can we then begin to rise a little above our fate. Then, but only then, everything somehow becomes possible, even surrender. And with surrender, something new within us may open up of itself. If we can then remain quiet and completely passive, something new and fine might enter.

5

Conciliatory Healing: Mind, Heart, and Spirit

In the center of the brain is an area called the hypothalamus. Researchers have learned, from experiments with animals, that the various sections of the hypothalamus are concerned with such things as sexuality, hunger, pleasure, pain, and all the emotions. In other words, if an electrode is used to stimulate a certain spot in the hypothalamus, the animal will display all the signs of fearful panic. Stimulation of a different spot will lead to all the signs of relaxed contentment. In fact, all our emotions and all our appetites appear to be clearly mapped out within the hypothalamus.

Just above the hypothalamus are the two enormous cerebral hemispheres. This part of the brain is the seat of the higher thinking functions. Damage to the cerebral hemispheres can lead to all sorts of problems with the senses, the voluntary movements, and the intellect. Thousands of nerves connect the hypothalamus to the cerebral hemispheres. Information is constantly being passed in both directions. Thus, the intellectual part of our brain is in constant communication with the emotional part of our brain.

Just below the hypothalamus, sitting right in the midst of the brain, is the pituitary gland. The pituitary gland is often called the "master" gland of the endocrine system. The pituitary tells all the other glands what to do: it tells the thyroid when to speed up the body's metabolism by producing more thyroid hormone, it tells the adrenals when to cut down the production of cortisone, and so on. The pituitary is thus like a master conductor, conducting the body's great chemical symphony.

But the hypothalamus *composed* the symphony, and is always rewriting parts of it. Under different intellectual and emotional conditions, the hypothalamus sends different signals to the pituitary, which in turn sends different instructions to the body regarding the production of hormones, those powerful chemical messengers that are sent via the bloodstream to every single cell of the body.

Here, then, is the direct link between mind, emotions, and body! Changes in thoughts and emotions will change the very chemistry of the blood itself through the influence of powerful yet delicate hormones, no doubt in many more ways than we have yet discovered or perhaps even imagined. Clearly, these physical results of our thoughts and emotions give us the possibility of changing the very content of our lifeblood and the very essence of each of our cells. Thus we are given the possibility of healing ourselves, by changing not just what we *do* but what we *feel* and what we *think*.

Two important questions now arise. First, in addition to the direct effects of our outward words and gestures, what indirect effects might the permeating vibrations given off by our thoughts and emotions have upon our physical bodies, upon other people, and possibly upon the planet? Second, consider the reproductive system. The formation and release of sperm and egg are controlled by sex hormones, which are controlled in turn by our thoughts and emotions. What unknown but critical effects might our internal states thereby have upon an individual fertilization and the resulting human child? Further, while developing in the womb, the child is fed by the mother's blood – blood whose chemical makeup is continuously being altered by the mother's thoughts and feelings.

Obviously we can heal ourselves. Obviously our lives have an effect on the people around us. Perhaps also, our thoughts and emotions even effect the totality of what we bequeath to our as yet unborn children.

MIND AND BRAIN

In the *New York Times* for 22 April 1986, a Washington University psychologist is quoted as saying that "the separation between mind and brain has seemed a bar to progress in psychology." In the same article, a psychologist from Harvard University is quoted as saying that "for the first time we have the concepts to guide us in looking at how the brain makes the mind, and the tools that allow us to look."

But does the brain make the mind?

We know that if we physically stimulate or damage the material of the brain, we will get corresponding changes in the content of our emotions and thoughts. This fact has led many researchers to assume that electrophysical events in the material of the brain "cause" emotions and thoughts. But there is actually no evidence whatsoever for this sort of clear-cut statement about causality. The only thing we know is that when there are certain physical events in our brain, there are simultaneously corresponding events in our psyche. But this fact only demonstrates synchronicity, the sameness-in-time of two events. It would be no more or less valid to assume that the thought causes the event in the brain, as to assume that the brain causes the thought. They are synchronous. There cannot be one without the other. But there is no evidence to demonstrate that either one must necessarily come first. If we artificially stimulate the brain, we will definitely have a simultaneous event in the mind. But it is equally true that if we first initiate an internal thought, we will have a simultaneous event in the brain!

One of the extraordinary realizations of modern physics is that we can look at an atom either as a grouping of individual particles or as a blending of interpenetrating vibrations. If we look at it as a combination of small material particles, we can devise and conduct experiments in which the atom demonstrates all the expected qualities of solid matter. But if we are determined to look at it as a field of vibrations, we can conduct other experiments in which the atom perfectly well demonstrates all the qualities of an immaterial energy wave. This "wave/particle duality" is a problem for two reasons. First, because according to our usual understanding of waves and particles they have no qualities or properties in common! Second, because our Newtonian science assumes that any subjective choice that the scientist makes internally must have no influence upon objective material reality. But the atoms, heedless of our assumptions, continue to display their "impossibly" paradoxical properties.

Apparently they are neither simply particles nor simply vibrations but something much vaster, which our limited way of looking at things cannot perceive as a whole. We only look at things from one level, believing that only one level of existence (our level, of course) is "real." We thus see contradictions where none exist, and like the medieval scholars who tried to find out how many angels can sit on the head of a pin, we argue and bicker and invent theories to explain imaginary external problems, when the problem is actually an internal one.

What, then, of "mind/brain duality"? Our mind and our brain are two synchronous ways of looking at one ineffable thing from two different levels of perception. And the same can be said of "mind/body duality." Rather than saying that our thoughts and emotions cause certain hormonal changes in the body, we again must only say that these two events occur synchronously on different levels. We exist on many levels. The job of science is to examine only that level to which its methods are applicable. Our total being, however—which even science admits has barely been tapped, and which includes many other magnificent qualities in addition to scientific rationalism (analytical thinking, analogical thinking, imagination, contemplation, reflection, artistic creativity, intuition, meditative states, instinct, physical expressiveness, emotional expressiveness, religious aspiration, etc.)—is potentially capable of experiencing and understanding many levels of existence. To say that we exist on many levels is very different than merely saying that we are many-sided. "Many-sided" is a horizontal statement. "Different levels" is a vertical statement. We are all many-sided. Moses, Jesus, and Buddha were also many-sided, but they lived on a very different level than you and I. Perhaps part of their message was to show us what higher levels of life are humanly attainable, and what efforts are required to reach them. Perhaps what a man or woman *knows* is not as important as what a man or woman *is*.

Carl Sagan makes the observation in his book *The Dragons of Eden* that the fact that science has not yet learned something does not mean that it will not learn it eventually. But he apparently assumes, without any rigorous justification, that all knowledge is on the same level, and that the rational part of our brain is the only thing necessary or qualified for comprehending the universe. He also assumes that the many successes of science have thereby proved its unquestionable claim to authority in all matters. This brings up the inherent problem with relying exclusively on science to satisfy our human need for understanding: that is, the difference between knowledge and understanding. Knowledge can be acquired by any of our faculties, including emotional knowledge, experiential knowledge, and, of course, the rational knowledge that Western science has brought to such heights. But *understanding* requires a balanced participation of *all* our faculties. It is only when knowledge blends with all parts of our being that it becomes genuine understanding. We typical modern Westerners are full of scientific knowledge, yet because we tend to neglect the rest of our being we are overwhelmed with inner contradictions, and all our knowledge has therefore brought us hardly any understanding. It is not that Sagan and his way of looking at things are illogical. But his narrow world of scientific perception and scientific logic, no matter how brilliant, is nonetheless severely limited. This lack of balanced reasoning eventually can lead to such reprehensibly upside-down conclusions as his matter-of-fact statement that "love seems to be an invention of the mammals."

I mention all of this because our overall psyche—by which term I mean all the possibilities of the mind, heart, and spirit—is the final arbiter of health and disease. It provides the third healing force, which either reconciles a poisonous substance and weak tissue to destruction, or reconciles a healing action and strong, receptive tissue to health. At all times our psyche is either suppressing our immune system or bolstering it by determining our hormone levels and determining the effectiveness of our disease-fighting white blood cells. Thus, it is only through attention to our mind, heart, and spiritual aspirations that we can complete a successful triad of healing.

What does all this information lead to? For one thing, it leads to the indisputable clinical observations of hypnosis, biofeedback, visualization, and meditation that our physiological healing powers can be harnessed and strengthened with these psychological exercises and techniques. For another thing, it leads to the conclusion that our overall psychology is a crucial factor in physical as well as mental disease, and that in-depth psycho-therapeutic work can be an important requirement for both prevention and healing. Next, it tells us that our inner, "invisible" life, our emotional, intellectual, and spiritual life, is as much a part of reality as the visible physical machine called the body and brain. It tells us that our loves and hates, our misery and happiness, our knowledge and ignorance, our apathy and aspiration, our wisdom and foolishness, our experience of self and experience of God—all of this matters.

For several hundred years the West has tended to neglect the state of our souls. Even some of our most committed reformers and humanitarians have been imbued with a soulless, Newtonian point of view. For all their well-meant efforts, without a soul the physical body and social environment inevitably devolve toward destruction and death. And one has to suppose that without a soul, this really makes no particular difference anyway. But perhaps we still have the seeds of a soul, and perhaps with attention to our inner as well as our outer life we can still turn ourselves and our world in the direction of health, life, and meaning.

HARNESSING THE HEALING PSYCHE

In his book *Anatomy Of An Illness,* Norman Cousins reflects as follows:

> Many medical scholars have believed that the history of medicine is actually the history of the placebo effect. Sir William Osler underlined the point by observing that the human species is distinguished from the lower orders by its desire to take medicine. Considering the nature of nostrums taken over the centuries, it is possible that another distinguishing feature of the species is its ability to survive medication. At various times and in various places, prescriptions have called for animal dung, powdered mummies, sawdust, lizard's blood, dried vipers, sperm from frogs, crab's eyes, weed roots, sea sponges, 'unicorn horns,' and lumpy substances extracted from the intestines of cud-chewing animals. . . . People were able to overcome these noxious prescriptions, along

with the assorted malaises for which they had been prescribed, because their doctors had given them something far more valuable than drugs: a robust belief that what they were getting was good for them. They had reached out to their doctors for help; they believed that they were going to be helped – and they were.[2]

Placebos were originally employed to verify the efficacy of an experimental drug. Researchers thought they were comparing the effects of a drug, as opposed to simply not taking anything at all. It was a great surprise to discover that placebos had effects of their own, effects that were markedly different from simply not taking anything: and not just in the realm of subjective complaints about pain, but in terms of actual changes in blood chemistry and tissue growth, and even remission and recovery from supposedly terminal diseases. We now know that the healing actions that are attributed to a drug can be brought about by the *belief* that one has taken the drug. This certainly raises some interesting questions about how our minds work. But what does it tell us about how *drugs* work?

The natural principles of the body can be studied and described by medical science. And along with the ability to describe the processes of the body comes the possibility of imitating them: anti-inflammatory drugs can imitate the work of adrenal hormones and prostaglandins, antibiotics can imitate the functions of white blood cells, diuretics can imitate the function of the kidneys. These drugs may act more rapidly, and even more forcefully, than is normally customary for the body. But at bottom they are still only ingenious inventions for imitating principles that have been learned from the body itself. And just as mothers have been known to lift trucks off their children's bodies at accident sites, so we know that it is quite possible, in times of great need, for our bodies to work with just as much rapidity and forcefulness as any drug.

The placebo effect is connected with our particular scientific worldview, and the fact that any effective healing art is a product of the knowledge, wishes, and beliefs of the people and culture within which it develops. Apparently the drug itself is not necessary. All that is required is our belief that scientists

have demonstrated the drug's usefulness: this allows our unconscious mind to turn on our innate, instinctive, body intelligence.
The drug itself is but a sop to our particular philosophical prejudices. For primal peoples, the exact same thing can be accomplished by chants and dances.

This may sound a bit extreme, but it is not all that much so.
There are certainly situations in which the chemical drug itself
takes over regardless of the patient's psychological state. But it is
indisputable that research into nutrition, stress, and especially
the placebo effect has demonstrated that toxic drugs and other
remedies are, ideally, not necessary. The ultimate conclusion to
be drawn from the fact of the placebo effect is not that pain and
illness are all in our heads, or that we are easily fooled. The
placebo effect does not belittle us. It empowers us. It tells us that
we have profound possibilities, and that we can take control of
our health. It reassures us that nature, though it can be cruel, is
willing to be on our side if only we put in some effort to cooperate. And it promises that we need never underestimate the
capacity of the human mind, heart, and body to heal.

Consider the fantastic implications of the following information from Bernie Siegel's book *Love, Medicine and Miracles,* in
which he discusses the results of studies of people with multiple
personalities: "One personality may be a diabetic, while the
other is not. Allergies and drug sensitivities may be present in
one personality, but not in others. If one personality burns the
body with a cigarette, the mark may disappear when the other
personality is in control and reappear when the first personality
reappears."[3] How can we take *deliberate* hold of this incredible
power? How can we tell our wounds to heal, our diseased organs
to repair themselves, our white blood cells to ingest a tumor?
"Basic techniques for contacting the unconscious mind and harnessing its powers have been a standard part of people's education in many cultures, especially in the East and in preindustrial,
tribal societies. . . ." In the West, such methods have been almost totally neglected in favor of logical processes."[4] It turns out,
however, that our bodies do not respond to logical words and
commands. But the body very definitely does respond to emotional feelings and, as we shall see, to **vivid pictorial images.**

Thus, it is through our feelings and through our imagination that we can learn to send deliberate healing instructions into our body.

Studies by Siegel and others[5] on the forefront of research into emotional effects on physical illness, have concluded that the two particular internal events that repeatedly predate and help to bring on serious illness are a feeling of powerlessness over one's life and the repression of negative feelings such as anger. They also conclude that the most important step in overcoming illness (in addition to taking control again, and learning to express one's honest needs and feelings) is the cultivation of forgiveness and love, both toward oneself and toward others. Now to make such a clear-cut statement is all well and good, but deep psychological change is never easy. In speaking briefly about these emotional considerations, I do not mean to undervalue the great courage and effort that is necessary even to begin to look at our inner thoughts and emotions without becoming judgmental or defensive. If we do not know or admit that we have a problem, it is impossible to change it! Learning to bear impartial witness to one's own mind is a step both formidable and magical.

FOUR EMOTIONAL ISSUES

Powerlessness and suppression of anger, forgiveness and love: these are the four basic emotional issues we must begin to consider in order to enhance the third force of healing.

Powerlessness means a failure to see all the possibilities. It is a way we sometimes react to stress, but it is never the only way open to us. One way to maintain power over our lives, and thereby to convince the unconscious mind that health is both desired and anticipated, is to take good care of ourselves: a diet of Twinkies and Coca-Cola is a sure sign that we have given up and no longer care. The most effective means to overcome powerlessness is to set an aim and to pursue it regardless of any obstacles. It is said that most of us do not get what we want out of life, simply because we never knew what it was we wanted. We become powerless when we are aimless. Having an aim and working to attain it gives us a reason for living, without which the unconscious mind has no particular reason to heal the body. An aim does not have to be grandiose; in fact, it has to be realistic. Even if we think we are too sick or too depressed to care, we can pretend there is something we want to accomplish and set out to do it. By keeping at it, it becomes real: one of the standard aphorisms of successful behavior is "Act as if." If we act as if we are in control of our lives, the unconscious mind will soon get the message and we will be in control. And people who have a clearly defined reason for living live longer and live better.

Carl Simonton and Stephanie Matthews-Simonton note that they believe we have developed our illnesses "for honorable reasons." Illness means that somewhere along the line our legitimate needs are not being met. These needs may be physical, sexual, emotional, psychological, social, or spiritual. If we are not meeting our serious needs appropriately, we may have to meet them artificially through disease. Much in our society opposes the fulfillment of normal human needs, and even tries to replace them with unnecessary things. To become healthy we must learn to distinguish our true needs from the effects of advertising and habit, and to answer them appropriately and joyously.

The realization that we have legitimate needs, that we are connected by a sacred system of give-and-take with other people and with the world, is a liberating realization. It means that we have the right and the obligation to ask. It means that we have the right and obligation to receive. It means that we have the right and obligation to give. The recognition that one has contributed to one's own ill health has nothing to do with assigning guilt or blame. This would totally miss the point. The point is that we do have power (there could not be an illness otherwise!), we do need other people, we do have a reason for living, and our illnesses occur for respectable reasons. The same internal forces that allowed disease to take hold can potentially be turned deliberately around and used for self-healing. There is immense power in this. In fact, there is really no such thing as powerlessness: it is just a question of whether our power works against us by default, or for us by conscious intent. By consciously and effectively taking care of ourselves, by working toward a goal, by clearly asking for help in meeting our needs, and by being there to help others meet their needs, we take back the power in our lives.

Certain seriously ill patients die faster than others. They are not the patients who are characteristically depressed and let everyone know about it: the latter reaction is negative and unhealthy, but at least such patients are acknowledging a part of their situation and showing some response to what is going on. It turns out that the patients who die the fastest are "the smiling ones who don't acknowledge their desperation, who say 'I'm fine' even though . . . their spouses have run off, their children are drug addicts, and the house just burned down."[6] Our body is evidently given a deadly message if we try to ignore our fears and anger. Anger is often a reasonable reaction if it is expressed cleanly when felt. Otherwise, it enters into the body and becomes extremely destructive.

We seem to live in a very nice society. Most of us are nice most of the time. Showing anger, hostility, hatred, and other less-than-nice emotions is generally frowned upon, and we exert a great deal of energy to control ourselves and appear nice.

It is nice to act nice when we feel nice. It can be deadly if we are actually furious. Naturally common sense is required: of course we must control the impulse to murder. But most impulses to murder will only arise when all the simpler impulses (such as anger) have been repressed by a delusionary niceness. Notice that underneath this nice society seethes a viciously violent society. We tend to surround our real selves with a societally acceptable shield of niceness, and if our negativity finally breaks down that shield from the inside, all those repressed emotions come bursting out as violence. (This is, of course, the same shield that prevents anything from coming in. It shows itself in the physical body as rigidity, in the heart as callousness, in the mind as narrowness, and in the spirit as meaninglessness.) We are violent because we are not real. For fear of the response that might come, we do not get angry when we really feel angry, and we do not say "I love you" when we really feel love.

Being more freely expressive with our genuine feelings and impulses never means being violent; it means being active in our lives and situations, it means struggling to become conscious of our innermost needs and feelings, it means becoming real about who and what we are. Martin Luther King reminded us repeatedly that nonviolence does not mean nonaction. On the contrary, his call was to nonviolent *action*. Dr. King was among the world's most loving and forgiving men, but he never pretended that everything was all right with the world, he never pretended that he was not angry, he always said what was on his mind, and his actions were filled with power. We can take this idea into our daily lives and see that although violence is a crime against nature that never has a place, actively expressing our real, powerful emotions does have a place. "Sometimes the kindest act is to express genuine anger," writes Dr. Barbara Counter, "to say no, to be firm, to demand what is right, to refuse to collude with lies, destructiveness and death."7 And it is a simple and ancient truism that if I cannot express genuine hatred, then I cannot express genuine affection. Without the power of our dark side our finer emotions degenerate into sentimentality, and our physical bodies may degenerate into illness. Cancer and arthritis in particular have been called "diseases of nice people," and Siegel and others confirm that dramatic improvements in health occur when we begin to express our feelings and to give some reasonable freedom to our impulses.

Not only do painful interpersonal events have an effect on our physical bodies, but we magnify the damage to our immune system every time we recall painful events that have never been resolved. "People who carry such resentments continually re-create the painful event or events in their heads. This may even go on long after the offending person has died."8 That "offending person," whether alive or dead, can do nothing to help our immune system. This help must come from within ourselves, and it comes in the form of forgiveness. Such forgiveness is not meant to deny genuine feelings of hurt and anger: if something needs to be said, it needs to be said. But then the resentment must end and forgiveness begin. We do not forgive people's evil. We forgive their weaknesses.

When trying to forgive someone, we often come up against some surprising realizations. Part of the resentment may be an unconscious resentment toward ourselves, for our own part in the original hurtful event. We may have to start by forgiving our *own* weaknesses. Another possibility is that we will find it difficult to forgive because in fact we use the resentment to justify an unending role as the powerless, abused victim, or to continue feeling sorry for ourselves. Don Juan Mateus, the Yaqui Indian medicine man, taught his disciple, Carlos Castaneda, that for a person to become stuck in self-pity there must be three previous conditions. First, there must be a refusal to accept any responsibility for oneself (None of this is my fault); second, there has to be an inflated sense of self-importance (I don't deserve this. After all, look at who I am); and finally, there must be a belief that one will live forever (I can waste all the time I want feeling this way).[9]

One way to begin getting over blame is to imagine ourselves in the other person's shoes, to imagine having to cope with all the circumstances of his or her life, and then to imagine having to listen to everything that person ever heard *us* say. We may find that there are times when we expect this other person to do things or to endure things that we ourselves would never put up with! Here is where we might begin to find the "same thing in ourselves" that usually accounts for why we dislike and blame the other person. If we can see the exact same thing in ourselves that we have been resenting others for, the whole situation can immediately and magically clear up. This is the best kind of forgiveness, for it leaves no hidden residue and it feeds no sense of superiority. But it is also the most difficult, since it is very hard to see anything wrong in ourselves.

To forgive, then, often precipitates a chance to look more closely into our own selves, to see what we are and what we wish to become. Forgiveness should not be taken condescendingly or sentimentally. To forgive takes strength, inner sincerity, an awareness of the common condition of man, and a determined wish to heal oneself and to help others heal.

"I am convinced," writes Bernie Siegel, "that unconditional love is the most powerful known stimulant of the immune system. If I told patients to raise their blood levels of immune globulins or killer T cells, no one would know how. But if I can teach them to love themselves and others fully, the same changes happen automatically. The truth is: love heals."[10]

There are many kinds of love: love of self, love of another, love of children, love of life, love of God (to name just a few). There are even many kinds of love of self, many kinds of love of another, and so forth. One kind of self-love is merely vanity and narcissism. But another has to do with gratitude, awe and respect for the miracle of one's life, and the willingness to perfect oneself and be of service. This latter kind of love gives life meaning, and it is certainly necessary for healing.[11]

Romantic love also includes many variations. Often, what we think is love of another is really a demand to *be* loved. Unfortunately, this kind of love seems to evoke mostly resentment, sooner or later, on the part of the beloved. It is at these times that we often become indignant, and say peculiar and inappropriate things like "After all the love I've given you . . . ," when little was given at all.

A more satisfying kind of love, but one which no doubt requires a Herculean effort to attain, is a love that honestly wishes for the happiness, well-being, and perfection of the beloved regardless of any results for oneself. This kind of love, I am told, always evokes the same kind of love. That is, a truly selfless love is, paradoxically, the best way to become the *recipient* of selfless love. To become realistically capable of this is a long and arduous internal task, and it is probably asking too much of any of us as we are. I venture these thoughts with no illusions about being personally able actually to reach this sacred level of love. But the enormous difficulty inherent in becoming the kind of man or woman who *can* attain this, is why the subject of love—which we so often take for granted and think we have mastered by the age of fourteen—should be the subject of a lifetime of contemplation.

Perhaps what is most missing in our Newtonian world is a love for anything *above* ourselves and each other. A few fundamentalists continue to think of God as a nasty old fellow who spends His time thinking up new ways to get even with us. But most of us have succeeded in explaining God away as some sort of mindless, passionless "energy," or as some quality of our known world such as its "totality" (by some marvelous miracle of modern thinking, we have now decided that everybody is God!), or else we have eliminated God altogether from our lives. I once heard someone very wise say that there is really not a question about whether God exists: the only question is whether we have an experience of God in our lives or not. Perhaps God is someone who can be talked to, questioned, argued with, yelled at, confided in, and sought after. Perhaps God has a wish for us, a purpose of His own, and perhaps God needs love too.

To be able to love is no easy feat. To assume one already knows how is to invite resentment and loneliness. Worse yet, to give up trying is to invite sickness and death. Love heals. Love creates the world.

MENTAL IMAGERY AND MEDITATION

The quickest way to begin to change our emotions and thus our physical health, is to employ the power of the imagination. The technique of mental imagery means creating mental pictures of desired states and events, concentratedly imagining them in utterly vivid detail, and repeating them internally over and over again. In many ways the unconscious mind apparently does not distinguish between actual events and events that have been vividly imagined. One of the most dramatic verifications of this (there are many) was an experiment a few years ago with young basketball players. One group of youths was asked to practice shooting baskets for an hour each day over a period of several weeks. A second group was told to stay off the court, but to spend an hour each day *imagining* that they were successfully shooting baskets, mentally going through all the motions and watching in their mind's eye as the ball left their fingertips and soared through the hoop. At the end of the experiment a competition was held. Everyone had improved, and those who had exercised only in imagination performed as well as those who had actually practiced on the court. Somehow, their muscle control, hand-eye coordination, aim, and overall skill had all improved simply by imagining the improvement.[12]

Imagery techniques have long been used in motivational psychology. A successful businessman is confident, friendly, decisive, and determined. By vividly imagining ourselves in possession of these qualities we can, over time, become truly imbued with them. The same techniques can imbue us with good health. "Mental imagery is not a method of self-deception," write the Simontons in *Getting Well Again.* "It is a method of self-direction."[13] By using such techniques to visualize the desired outcome *as if* it were already so, the patient takes a conscious and effective step in helping to *make* it so.

Thus it is possible to install an image of health into the body that the body must then reach for. In time, every cell and molecule will strive to realize the new blueprint. And just as our consciousness can use the language of images to *send* instructions, so perhaps it is possible to quiet the mind, to relax the musculature, and to *listen* with the heart. By focusing our attention on a particular problem and asking for help, perhaps we can also *receive* images. If we are then willing to trust what the unconscious tells us and to do what is asked, we may raise self-healing another immeasurable notch.

A further practice that can be of inestimable use in promoting health and wholeness is that of meditation. Again and again, people who begin to meditate discover not only that their health improves, but that all aspects of their lives are affected in beneficial ways.

If you sit quietly with a relaxed body, and then just try to be silent and passive, you can watch the thoughts float by: "I'd like a baked potato with dinner, how long have I been sitting here, my nose itches, what he said wasn't very nice, what time is dinner tonight, I have to finish that report before tomorrow's meeting, all this pressure has me in a bad mood, I think she likes me, I'm really having an interesting experience now, I can't stand that guy, maybe a mashed potato would be better, this is so boring, she's so cute, I should do this *twice* a day, french fries sounds good, did I remember to lock the car, I know what I should have told him, what's on TV tonight, am I relaxed now?" Meditation is an attempt to temporarily silence this constantly chattering mind, the mind that is endlessly busy talking about nothing while the time of our life gradually disappears.

Meditation can have extraordinary effects on physical and emotional health. "It tends to lower or normalize blood pressure, pulse rate, and the levels of stress hormones in the blood. It produces changes in brain-wave patterns, showing less excitability. These physical changes reflect changes in attitude, which show up on psychological tests as a reduction in the competitive type A behavior that increases the risk of heart attack. Meditation also raises the pain threshold and reduces one's biological age. . . . In short, it reduces wear and tear on both body and mind, helping people live better and longer."[14]

Meditation, like relaxation, is not easy for most of us. It is often necessary to take a class or to receive some sort of instruction. One approach to learning how to meditate is to focus one's attention on one's breathing: counting breaths from one to ten, then one to ten again, repeating this over and over again. At first, just try to maintain this for a few minutes each day. As other thoughts float by (and they will), it is important not to try forcibly to repress them. Rather, just try to notice them indifferently and let them go, without responding to them, without getting caught up in an internal conversation with them. We can begin to see here that our thoughts are just thoughts, they are not "us," and we do not necessarily have to identify with them or have our attention swept away by them. In the quiet of meditation we can remember what *is* us, what is permanent, solid, and ours, rather than always being lost somewhere amid what is transient, external, and superficial, which has infected us from TV, advertising, other people's prejudices, and automatic inner voices that we would not especially like or even recognize if we stopped for a moment and listened.

Learning to meditate does not mean learning to be stupid or unemotional. When thinking is called for, the power of concentration (which both imagery and meditation can teach us) can help our thinking to be precise, logical, and penetrating, just as it can help our emotions to be genuine, passionate, and powerful. To enhance the active force of healing, we need to take control of our thoughts and emotions in just this way. To enhance the receptive force of healing, we must also learn to still our body, heart, and mind.

As imagery is active and meditation is passive, so prayer is conciliatory. Healing requires a balance of all three forces. Without prayer, or the act of making a connection to something higher, we can end up using imagery merely to acquire riches, or meditation merely to obtain a "far-out" experience of peacefulness. In themselves, there is nothing wrong with either of these goals. On the contrary, they are of great potential value. But *by* themselves they are so unbalanced, so ultimately worthless. They merely become contributors to a banal self-aggrandizement and self-interest, replacing any meaningful effort at self-perfection. Imagery and meditation require a purpose in order to be truly valuable. That purpose is not to be found in the means themselves, or in any subjective, groundless presumption of our own choosing. We cannot invent true purpose or meaning. We discover them in our aspiration to a level higher than ourselves.

Psychological work today generally places people in the center of all things, relegating anything higher to a "characteristic" within our minds (rather than the reverse). This outlook comes directly from our Newtonian view that all things can be understood without recourse to anything above. When Pierre Laplace presented Napoleon with his five-volume work *Mecanique Celeste*, in which he had refined Newton's system to explain the heavenly motions down to the smallest detail, the emperor is reported to have remarked that he was surprised to receive a book on the system of the universe that included no mention of its Creator. Laplace replied bluntly, "I had no need of that hypothesis." But it is not at all impossible, as Eugene Bewkes suggests, that "the laws of nature are an expression of intelligence, not a mechanical result of matter in motion," and that "the order of nature is meaningful, concerned with rational goals and values."[15] In the preface to this book I raised the possibility that mankind might have an obligation to the earth, perhaps even somehow to the sun or to yet higher powers. Perhaps these are our *real* parents, and our psychological examination of ourselves must include a thorough analysis of our relationship to *them*.

The methods discussed here are more powerful than any treatment, any drug, or any invention of man. The will to live, the applied power of the imagination, and an unshakable aim are among the most powerful forces in the universe. A body, mind, and heart that can achieve self-control and inner stillness are capable of anything. And the strongest defense against disease, indeed the strongest defense against all of life's horrors, is a body, mind, and heart filled with love. Not sentimental love, not sitting-on-a-mountainside-smiling-like-a-zombie love, not weak, clingy love. Love is vibrant, often angry, it aspires to perfection for the lover and the beloved, it finds its inspiration in the highest and the holiest, and it is always powerful.

THE NEED FOR MEANING

Because we have elevated science to a position of unparalleled authority, we tend to surrender our personal search for truth and meaning to the scientists, expecting that these experts will supply us with the necessary and accurate answers. But science does not ask "What does it mean to be a human being?" or "What is the reason for my life?" Science and its companion, realism, cannot be dismissed: but they can and must be questioned. And what is impossible for material science is not necessarily impossible for a human being. Technology has not provided us with a satisfactory explanation for our lives. We have to look elsewhere.

Allan Bloom, in his devastating book *The Closing of the American Mind*,[16] points out that the United States was established upon two great principles: freedom and equality. The principle of freedom, for the Founding Fathers, primarily meant freedom of *thought*—the freedom to pursue knowledge, truth, and wisdom without any religious or political constraints. American society was to be built in such a way that this freedom was guaranteed and the quest for human fulfillment encouraged. But what has resulted, instead, is a new definition of freedom which now has to do with freedom from any sort of unwanted responsibility: "I don't have to do anything I don't want to do, because *I've got my rights.*" The theory of the inalienable rights of man, with which the nation's founders were concerned, was nature's guarantee that we could explore the soul and the universe unencumbered, that as individuals and as a community we could discover the best and finest life. Now these rights have become little more than a rationalization for license. The only constraint we still have left on our behavior is the vague rule that what we do must not present "a clear and present danger." That is, as Americans we believe that the greatest moral imperative is that we have the right to do whatever we want to do, so long as it does not hurt anyone else. One inevitable result of this is that the maintenance of public order becomes the only common aim, rather than the pursuit of what is true and good for individuals and society. But this interpretation of freedom's intent is recent. As Bloom points out, Abraham Lincoln insisted that in order to fulfill the promise of the Constitution the slaves had to be emancipated, that this was necessary because it was right, in spite of a "clear and present danger" of civil war!

Equality and Relativism

Equality, the other great American principle, originally meant that all citizens, so long as they obeyed the law, had to be treated fairly no matter how distasteful their beliefs or customs might be: all Americans were to have equal access to worldly success and human fulfillment, without regard to any unequal conditions of family status or inherited abilities. Today, however, this principle of equality has been confused with the idea that everything is equal in *value:* differences in value, we assume, are only a matter of personal opinion, and no one ought to have the audacity to claim that his or her opinion is better than anyone else's. Everything must be accepted in a spirit of utter tolerance, and the greatest moral crime would be to assume that any ideas or beliefs are more true than any other. Thus, everything is *relative* in America today. With moral zeal, we admit no possibility that anything might in itself be genuinely true, good, or right. It is therefore an unrealistic waste of time to ask serious questions. What is the purpose of life? Whatever I want it to be. Is there a God? If I say so. Since truth, like everything else, is relative, we might just as well switch from the national pursuit of truth to the more comfortable pursuit of utility.

It is now generally believed that America stands for just this sort of openness to anything, whereas America originally stood for very distinctive and purposeful principles. The moral ground for our society used to be the inalienable rights of all men and women. Now the moral ground has become our national recognition of the relative *sameness* of all men and women, and the relative sameness of all thoughts, principles, and values. This bland sameness, with its implied denial of anything substantive or noble, has emptied our souls of any inherent meaning or worth, and this condition is the underlying sickness of which all our more obvious ills are only effects. What was once sacred has now become nothing more than a shallow hobby for a few eccentrics, a pointless historical study for a few disinterested scholars, or a quick way to make a buck for a few charlatans. Serious people have no time, need, or interest in this. Acquisition has become the legitimate replacement. In the meantime, unisexual passionless "significant others" have replaced real men and women. The heroes, villains, geniuses, conquerors, lovers, and saints of the past are now better understood to have been unsophisticated folks who could have benefited greatly from the proper therapy. Love of neighbor has been replaced by a condescending "acceptance of life-style." And the soul, with all its potential depth, has been replaced by the "self" and all its unpleasant neuroses. "It is not the immorality of relativism that I find appalling," Bloom comments. "What is astounding and degrading is the dogmatism with which we accept such relativism, and our easygoing lack of concern about what that means for our lives."[17]

Newtonian science supports this casual, philosophical relativism by insisting that both we and our universe are nothing more than machines, accidents of evolution; and science can offer no indisputable evidence that we are necessarily of any more ultimate value than a good VCR. Finally, we suppose that history, with its changing fashions and moralities, with its wars, crusades, inquisitions, and slaughters, sufficiently demonstrates that all beliefs and cultures are relative, and that it is far too dangerous to think that any are more right than any others.

The kind of openness that we have accepted as a great virtue is really just indifference. We approve of this indifference because it safely and comfortably respects everyone else's opinions, no matter how brilliant or ridiculous, and because it promises us in return that we can do anything we please. But the consequence of such indifference is that we become the slaves of fashion and whim, and can be counted upon to rally in support of whoever or whatever is the most popular or powerful of the day. Tolerance of everything leaves us indifferently ready to surrender to anything. We become bored, submissive, unhappy, and unhealthy, and we become a danger to ourselves, to one another, and to posterity.

The Pursuit of Wisdom

A higher form of openness recognizes the complexities and possibilities that are always present in the deepest human questions and longings, and it recognizes the human need to search for certitude and wisdom. For the pursuit of these questions we have been blessed with sublime sources of information and ideas that can be probed and pondered. But in our scientific era, with our boundless faith in progress and our smug contempt for the past, we tend to discount the possibility of any real, relevant value in the Bible, Homer, Shakespeare, Dante, Plato, the Upanishads, the Koran, and so on. We view these things simply as interesting artifacts of romantic, bygone days. Worse yet, they are filled with such unenlightened attitudes as sexism, imperialism, and religion, and thereby forfeit any lingering claim to our respect. We glance briefly at selected excerpts from these works during our school years, relate to them our own instant opinions and assumptions, and seek nothing from them but some passing entertainment. Then we move on to our more important functions in the adult world. These works are just a part of history. And in our stressful, important, day-to-day lives, who really cares about that?

For most of us, the Bible is just a quaint source of presophisticated moralism, or at best an interesting example of a particular type of literature that is no longer popular. Amid all its savagery, sexism, and sentimental platitudes, there is surely nothing of any practical importance for a serious, modern American. It is only important historically. A scholarly historian, earnestly concerned with figuring out where society began to go wrong and how we might now reset a more promising course, can find in a superficial reading of the Bible hundreds of examples of dangerous wrong-thinking that can now be corrected with the tools of science, psychology, and sociology. But instead of easily presuming that the Bible is "wrong," that we understand what it is saying but are compelled to disagree, perhaps it would be interesting to suppose – hypothetically – that we do not understand what it is saying at all, and that a fresh study might yield some surprisingly new and relevant ideas.

Occasionally, after staring incomprehendingly for many days at one or another biblical passage, after posing questions about it to people much smarter than myself, and after despairing of ever understanding anything again, occasionally a tiny light turns on and – like a gift – a slightly new way of thinking about something becomes possible. When this happens, I can begin to grasp with a warm feeling of awe how it was that my great-grandfather, like so many people of his generation and those before him, would never go out in the morning until he had spent time studying the Torah. I used to imagine that such a ritual was an imposition, unfairly placed upon him by a medieval sense of duty which I, fortunately, was too modern and free to be burdened with. But with the one or two very minor insights that I feel I have recently discerned, and the feelings of intellectual, emotional, and spiritual excitement that they arouse in me, I begin to envy my great-grandfather's freedom to pursue truth every day of his life – a freedom that I am ill-prepared for, and in any case usually too busy to take.

One area that provides some interesting food for thought is the subject of sexual roles. The history of civilization does indeed appear to be a history of male domination, as many modern scholars have pointed out to us. Among the causes of this domination, at least apparently, are various statements in the Judeo-Christian Bible. In modern times we have realized that these statements are mistaken and unfair, that men and women are equal. In light of this recognition, I recently attended a synagogue service in which every reference to "Abraham, Isaac and

Jacob" was replaced by "Abraham and Sarah, Isaac and Rebeccah, Jacob and Rachel and Leah." But this sort of didactic change in response to public pressure is not a solution to our problems. It is merely a tiresome compromise that tells us nothing about the distinctive roles of either the patriarchs or the matriarchs.

As we have seen, contemporary American society is embarked on a quest to equalize everything. From jobs to domestic duties to unisex haircuts, everyone is supposed to be the same. Only biology differentiates us, and biology is not destiny. Everything else that apparently differentiates us is no more than the deplorable result of societal conditioning due to past misunderstanding of the equality (read "sameness") of the sexes. The feminist claim of abuse is undeniably valid. But two equivalent jobs and an equal sharing of household duties is not a solution: it is, again, only a compromise. And it is a compromise that fails. We can legislate equal rights, and we can insist on equal sentiments, but if nature does not cooperate then all these steps are in vain. I am not suggesting that the old family situations were perfectly all right or that we should try to reinstate them. I only wish to point out that the quest for sameness has brought us at least as many unhappy, unfulfilled people as we had before. Domination did not work, and now sameness does not work. If there is a right relationship possible between the sexes, we have not found it.

The effort to correct the relationship between the sexes falls under the banner of *equality*. The sexual revolution was connected with our other great national principle, *freedom*. Repressive Victorian sexual ethics brought us nothing but problems, but it turns out that the sexual mores of the 1960s have brought us even worse problems. Sex used to be difficult but important. Now it is easy and boring. Making sex easy, readily available without the need for any emotional investment, trivialized it. Sex became "no big deal." This passionlessness is a devastating effect of the sexual revolution.

Lurking behind all the cruel and farcical differences that we have presumed to exist between men and women, there sits the ominous biblical accusation that women are evil. After all, they got us thrown out of the garden of Eden, and I for one will never forgive them. How could I? It seems to me that they are still doing the same thing, if on a somewhat smaller scale. Every time I have some self-styled noble purpose to pursue (peace on earth, say, or justice for all, or some such meritorious attempt to tend God's garden), what is the surest way to make me completely forget about my noble purpose? Of course: just let a lovely woman in a miniskirt walk by and I have quite forgotten all about it. Let her smile at me and tempt me to follow her, and I am done for. And the miserable unfairness of it all is that once I follow her, once I give up my own aims in order to spend every waking moment adoring her and indulging her every wish, then I soon become far too uninteresting to warrant any further attention. There I was, minding my own business and nobly tending the garden, and she tempted me away, and now she says the spark is gone!

Could the story of Adam and Eve have something to tell modern men and women about such things? Perhaps it is not just a deceptive old myth about how an evil woman ruined some ancient paradise. Maybe it is a story of how paradise must be *earned*, rather than simply given. Maybe humanity has a greater task, a greater responsibility, than tending the garden of Eden. But the garden was so pleasant and comfortable and blissful, that the Adam in us would be quite willing to waste an entire lifetime there. But Eve realized that Adam had to be drawn out of paradise in order to fulfill his purpose. Rather than throwing an infantile temper tantrum, as most men have done for thousands of years, blaming Eve for spoiling all the fun, it could be that Adam was *grateful* to Eve for saving him from eternal mediocrity. Perhaps the Bible is suggesting that a man needs a woman, to get his head out of the clouds (or out of the garden), and to get on with life.

Perhaps every Eve has to tempt every Adam, to see what sort of stuff he is made of. Maybe a woman has to know if a man is strong enough to balance desire with self-esteem, love with purposefulness. Maybe Adam was tempted and fell, just as we all have been tempted and fallen, and perhaps a deeper study of his story could help a man understand himself better, understand women better, and learn how to be both more loving and more manly.

Could it be that the idea behind what we have mistakenly interpreted as "evil" and overladen with so many horrible connotations, might simply be that Eve – for all the right reasons – *had* to turn Adam's attention away from God and back down to earth? Without this help, Adam might have remained as he was forever: a starry-eyed dreamer who did not know how to achieve his dreams. Without a woman in his life, and without a concurrent understanding of the "feminine" within his own psyche (which a real flesh-and-blood woman may have to lead him to and teach him about), perhaps a man is incapable of learning *how* to achieve his deepest aims and dreams. Likewise, without a man in her life, and a concurrent understanding of her own "masculine" aspect, perhaps a woman risks becoming aimless and "earthbound," because there is incomplete influence to remind her of *why*, to inspire her to *dream*.

These few reflections are not meant to define the final differences between men and women, and they are certainly not meant to imply that I have any noteworthy understanding of the endless levels of meaning and wisdom that lie hidden within the Bible. They are only mentioned in the hope that we, as a society, in the face of all the social upheaval we are experiencing, can begin seriously to ponder what it means to be a man, what it means to be a woman, and what relationship we ought actually to have with one another. And it is also my belief that the richness of living thought that lies ignored in the literary, philosophical, and religious tradition of the West (as well as that of the East) must be drawn upon once again to help us with this effort.

The Value of the Past

It is certainly possible that the great works of the past, the teachings that civilization was raised on, may contain some ideas that we would now, upon sincere reflection, wish to discard. The past was certainly not blameless. But we have to be wary of throwing out the baby with the bathwater. And this requires a reevaluation (and a revaluation) of education, both in the home and in our schools.

We usually believe that our parents and ancestors were uneducated and ignorant by our standards. Yet their homes were often emotionally, intellectually, and spiritually rich to a degree unheard of today, partly because there was no television or easy access to travel, but mostly because they were grounded in tradition, because their common stories and heroes gave them reasons for living, for working, for caring for each other. In Allan Bloom's words:

> I do not believe that my generation, my cousins who have been educated in the American way, all of whom are M.D.'s or Ph.D.'s, have any comparable learning. When they talk about heaven and earth, the relations between men and women, parents and children, the human condition, I hear nothing but clichés, superficialities, the material of satire . . . Without the great revelations, epics and philosophies as part of our natural vision, there is nothing to see out there, and eventually little left inside.[18]

This emptiness inside us is deadly. Cut off from the past, we are cut off from each other and cut off from the future. The profound sense of meaninglessness that results provides a most effective conciliatory cause in the triad of disease, both for individuals and for our society. Science has given us a great deal, but it does not satisfy our deepest needs. Realism is just an easy way out, and it clearly does not work. But within both the Western and Eastern traditions, much living richness can still be used to make some sense of our lives. Our health and our future depend upon this.

Past and Present

One practical problem to which our low opinion of the past leads is the cult of youth. The accompanying contempt for age not only impoverishes us by denying us the wisdom of experience and convincing us that only our personal here-and-now is important, but in its most terrible extreme can lead to an oversimplified notion of what makes life worth living and a breakdown of moral barriers to discarding people we choose to deem useless.

In an article in the *Village Voice* on 8 September 1987, Nat Hentoff discusses this dangerous trend. In 1920, he recalls, a book entitled *Consent to the Extermination of Life Unworthy To Be Lived* was published in Germany. Then, in 1939, according to Dr. Leo Alexander, who served with the office of the Chief Counsel for War Crimes in Nuremberg, "All state institutions were required to report on patients who had been ill five years or more and who were unable to work . . . The decision regarding which patients should be killed was made entirely on the basis of this brief information by expert consultants." Hentoff adds that the Holocaust "began with the mass killing of the old, the feeble-minded, the chronically ill, and those with multiple sclerosis, Parkinsonism, and brain tumors. Also severely handicapped children. Unwanted, 275,000 of them were exterminated. This was a dress rehearsal for the annihilation of six million Jews and millions of others."

Commenting some forty years later on the growing acceptance of euthanasia in America, Dr. Alexander said, "It is much like Germany in the 20's and 30's. The barriers against killing are coming down." Hentoff describes a "chill" he felt when reading a 1987 newsletter from a Society for the Right to Die, in which they reported data not unlike the information that Hitler required in 1939: "There are about three million Americans over the age of 85 and the number is rapidly growing . . . Most suffer ailments and require help in several activities of daily living. Some 50% are mentally or decisionally impaired to some degree."

Certainly, this information was not gathered in the same spirit as was Hitler's. But without a clear and solid philosophical groundwork of ethics and morals, which our relativism claims is nonexistent, to what use might this kind of information be put? A recent ruling by a seven-member council on ethical and judicial affairs of the American Medical Association has declared it ethical for physicians to withhold life-prolonging treatments if a patient is in a coma that "is beyond doubt irreversible and there are adequate safeguards to confirm the accuracy of the diagnosis." But when is anything besides death and burial irreversible beyond doubt? And who can be certain of the correctness of a diagnosis when countless autopsy studies and the abundance of malpractice cases prove conclusively that diagnostic mistakes are made all the time? Dr. Norman Levinsky, chief of medicine at Boston University Medical Center, told Hentoff that the AMA ruling "gives doctors and other care-givers a message that it's ok to kill the dying and get it over with. . . . Also, it is not a huge step from stopping the feeding to giving the patient a little more morphine to speed up his end. I mean, it is not a big step from passive to active euthanasia."

Some people, subjected to a long, protracted death filled with humiliation and pain, wish to be allowed to die with dignity. I am not suggesting that they have no such right, or that this is an easy issue to resolve. Quite the contrary, I agree with Hentoff that it is a very difficult and danger-laden issue, one that requires much more serious consideration than we have given it. It is an example of how we prefer to turn over our moral responsibilities to the scientists: "Let seven members of the AMA decide." And it is a warning of what can happen when we turn our backs to the whole tradition of sound, moral, responsible reasoning. For there is no question, adds Dr. Levinsky, "that some physicians and other care-givers consider the life of someone over 80 to be less worthy than that of someone who is 28."

In her celebrated book *On Death and Dying,* Dr. Elisabeth Kübler-Ross relates this story:

> I remember as a child the death of a farmer. He fell from a tree and was not expected to live. He asked simply to die at home, a wish that was granted without question. He called his daughters into the room and spoke with each one of them alone for a few minutes. He arranged his affairs quietly. . . . He asked his friends to visit him once more, to bid goodbye to them.[19]

This sort of death scene is in sharp contrast with our experience today, in which dying "becomes lonely and impersonal because the patient is often taken out of his familiar environment and rushed to the emergency room." Kübler-Ross goes on to point out that our frenetic and technical way of dealing with death is related, on the one hand, to our trend toward treating people as things, and on the other hand to our fear of death and our unwillingness to calmly and directly confront it, discuss it, and acknowledge it.

Along with this common fear, Kübler-Ross writes that it is evidently inconceivable for our conscious mind to imagine an actual ending to our own life. The mind simply cannot picture or believe in its own death, since in trying to do so it inescapably remains as a spectator. "If all of us would make an all-out effort to contemplate our own death, to deal with our anxieties surrounding the concept of our death, and to help others familiarize themselves with these thoughts, perhaps there could be less destructiveness around us."[20]

Perhaps this inability to remember that we are going to die is at the root of our difficulty in finding the strength and will to protect our health, our fellow beings, and our planet. If we unconsciously believe that we are going to live forever, there is no compelling reason to change. In *Journey to Ixtlan,* Carlos Castaneda describes a conversation with his spiritual guide, don Juan Mateus. Don Juan wants his pupil to see that he must make every moment count passionately, since life only lasts a short while. When Carlos claims that he is already doing all he can, don Juan replies:

"You're wrong again. You can do better. There is one simple thing wrong with you—you think you have plenty of time. . . . You think your life is going to last forever."

"No. I don't."

"Then, if you don't think your life is going to last forever, what are you waiting for? Why the hesitation to change?"

"Has it ever occurred to you, don Juan, that I may not want to change?"

"Yes, it has occurred to me. I did not want to change either, just like you. However, I didn't like my life; I was tired of it, just like you. Now I don't have enough of it."

I vehemently asserted that his insistence about changing my way of life was frightening and arbitrary. . . .

"You don't have time for this display, you fool," he said in a severe tone. "This, whatever you're doing now, may be your last act on earth. . . . There is no power which could guarantee that you are going to live one more minute."

"I know that," I said with contained anger.

"No. You don't. . . ."

I contended that I was aware of my impending death but it was useless to talk or think about it, since I could not do anything to avoid it. Don Juan laughed and said I was like a comedian going mechanically through a routine.

"If this were your last battle on earth, I would say that you are an idiot," he said calmly. "You are wasting your last act on earth in some stupid mood."

We were quiet for a moment. My thoughts ran rampant. He was right of course.

"You have no time, my friend, no time. None of us have time," he said.

"I agree, don Juan, but—

"Don't just agree with me," he snapped. "You must, instead of agreeing so easily, act upon it. Take the challenge. Change."[21]

PART 3

HEALING THE PLANET

I once attended a conference on the planetary dilemma. There were several speakers on the panel with backgrounds in biology, psychology, environmental science, sociology, medicine, physics, and religion. They all spoke intelligently and with great concern about the mess we humans are in, offering cogent analyses and practical suggestions. They sometimes disagreed with each other, but always in a spirit of cooperation and respect.

In the latter part of the day much was said about the fact that the planet earth shows many of the qualities of a living organism, and that if we continue to treat it destructively it will die. The message from all these speakers representing many different fields of endeavor was that the earth is not merely a mass of rock, hurtling through space with us as passengers, but is in fact a huge living organism, with us as part of a vast, interdependent ecology. The "planetary dilemma" is due to our poor treatment of this great ecological system. And the panel called upon us all to take better care of the earth.

As the conference neared its conclusion, comments were taken from the floor. At one point a little girl, perhaps nine years old, took the microphone and asked a question to this effect: "I have been listening all day about all these terrible things people do to the earth. But what I don't understand, and wish someone would tell me, is *why* – why do people do these things?"

This question, to my mind, was the only really important thing that had been said all day! Needless to say, it was quickly passed over—a story of dubious relevance was told by one of the panelists, and then the subject was quickly changed. All day long there had been *answers:* clever, educated, well-meant answers. But nobody, except this little girl, had any urgent questions! And yet, if we really had any worthwhile answers, we surely would not be in this mess.

Throughout the conference I marveled at everyone's self-satisfied intelligence. Every point was well made, every suggestion a good one. But what was lacking, it seemed to me, was an appreciation of levels. It was all such horizontal thinking. Much was made of the idea that the earth is alive, but the only conclusion that this led to was that the earth is a big, physical creature, kind of like a gigantic microbe, and we should take better care of it. Yet if the earth is alive, might it not have *all* the qualities of life? In addition to having a physical body, might it not also have a heart and mind? Being infinitely greater and older than any of us, perhaps the earth is actually much more evolved than we are: not merely a living "organism," but a living *being.* And perhaps, rather than talking condescendingly about our taking care of her, as if of a huge, ungainly child, perhaps it would be wiser to think that if we don't knock it off, she's going to get really angry!

6

The Present State
of Affairs

Healing is an all-encompassing process. It touches every aspect of our lives. And because our lives are part of all that lives, we cannot accurately call ourselves healed while others are suffering. Illness anywhere is a tear in the common fabric of life.

A book on healing may seem an unlikely place to discuss social or ecological issues. But surely the gravest threats to human health come in the form of environmental pollution and the possibility of a nuclear holocaust. How we deal with these matters, or why we fail to deal with them, is already a telling measure of our overall health.

It comes to this: the art of forgetting has become an essential part of our lives. By forgetting, we become comfortable with ourselves and our situation. We forget any sense of personal emptiness. We forget the sufferings of other people. This insidious comfort does indeed bring with it a certain form of happiness. But such happiness, in the midst of meaninglessness and the threat of extinction, is surely nauseating. And none of the accoutrements of this happiness (money, sexual adventure, social status, and the like) ever quite work: because no matter how physically or emotionally comfortable they make us feel, they can never quite overcome the discomfiting suspicion of inner nullity, or the conscience-pricking fear that we have forgotten to do something.

Notwithstanding our attempts to forget, we all know that greed, hatred, and apathy are threatening our individual lives, our society, and our planet. What keeps us from changing this? It is as if, deep within us, we carry an odious, hidden secret—

hidden even from our own selves: the secret that we are not merely willing to give it all up, but are in fact rushing toward our own final destruction. Something, within our unconscious, wants us to die. The politicians, the industrialists, the chemical companies, the military, and the criminals are not different from any of us. They are part of us. They are simply the agents for carrying out our own program, the one we have set for our own death. Because death will relieve our blandness and boredom, it will cleanse the emotional pain and loneliness, it will end our burdensome responsibilities, and it will justify our irresponsibility. Being alive means taking responsibility—for ourselves, for one another, for the world, and for the future. But the passion to do that is becoming harder and harder to find. Our secret longing for death, the devil within, is winning. And he is winning with incomparable ease.

Certainly it would be pointless and unhealthy to dwell on too much negativity about our political or ecological predicament. A positive attitude would carry us further toward solutions, but only if we are aware and informed. Otherwise, a "positive attitude" simply helps us to comfortably forget, while leaving us pathetically vulnerable to all the evil forces it denies. We cannot allow a self-indulgent, morbid negativity to poison us further by masquerading as the whole truth; but neither can we allow mere sentimentality to obscure harsh realities. We have to *earn* the right to be hopeful.

In *The Fate Of The Earth,* Jonathan Schell provides a gruesome description of a nuclear attack.[1] Even as he recognizes that it is difficult to read such an account, he also writes that only by descending now through imagination into this hell can we hope to escape entering it in reality later on. To end the poisoning and prevent a holocaust is going to require a deliberate psychological turn from comfortable forgetting to responsible remembering. This does not mean that we must only remember the repugnant. We must also remember the exquisite joy of being alive. But this, too, must be earned. In the meantime, is it really too much to ask that we try to save our world?

Consider what it cost nature to prepare this planet for human habitation: the aeons of growth and decay, experimentation, and change, so that we might have the possibility to live. And what do we do in return? "We behave in the family of Nature" – writes A. R. Orage – "like self-indulgent children whose only object is to enjoy ourselves. If you will only ponder seriously for half an hour on the way we exploit natural resources, land, forests, and animals, for the gratification of abnormal desires, you cannot help but be appalled."[2] We pride ourselves in being scientific. At the very least, science requires evidence. Where is the evidence that our exploitative behavior is somehow advantageous? Where is the evidence that we have a right to rape the earth? What *does* the evidence say?

A quarter century ago Rachel Carson observed that "given time – time not in years but in millennia – life adjusts, and a balance has been reached. For time is the essential ingredient; but in the modern world there is no time."[3] Our bodies, and all the other forms of life on the planet, are now expected to adapt to hundreds of strange new chemicals each year, chemicals that are totally outside the limits of evolutionary experience. We are told that these substances have been "tested and proven safe," a comforting half-truth that overlooks two crucial facts. First, there simply is no possible way to prove the long-term safety of any substance that continually accumulates in our tissues. Second, there exists no means of testing for potential *interactions* among so many new and uncontrollable factors in the environment.

Still, it is sometimes necessary, even wise, to balance the possibility of unknown problems against the likelihood of wonderful benefits. So we have to discuss the alleged benefits that we have received from modern chemical technology. The major benefits claimed are an increase in food production, a decrease in human disease, and a greater prosperity for all men and women. We need to examine these claims.

Since the first release of synthetic pesticides, the most striking thing we have gotten for our trouble is a viciously out-of-control escalation of chemical warfare, whereby the target insects mutate into resistant superspecies, and the chemists respond automatically by developing ever-deadlier chemicals. No miracle poison will finally rid our world of insect pests. They just keep evolving, and we just keep poisoning our own environment.

A teaspoon of soil contains billions of bacteria and other microbes. Many of these microbes are necessary for breaking down dead plants so that the soil remains rich in nutrients. Other microbes are needed to trap nitrogen and minerals in vegetable foodstuffs, where we can utilize them. The soil also contains earthworms, whose digging and tunneling brings life-sustaining air into the soil and makes possible the appropriate absorption and drainage of rainwater. Chemicals that are poisonous to a particular pest are also usually poisonous to many of these necessary life-forms and to their food supplies. The result is that we quickly rob the soil of its organic properties, creating thousands of acres of man-made deserts, which help to starve the poor of the earth. The thin crucial layer of the earth's topsoil maintains a fragile balance. Every activity of every inhabitant counts. In the United States alone, 3 billion tons of topsoil are being lost each year.

Early farmers had few insect problems. Simply by virtue of the wondrous variety of life forms in the earth's natural habitats, the populations of different species were kept in normal balance by competition for food, by predatory behavior, and by requirements of space. Farmers learned from this and mixed many crops and animals. When a vast section of land is covered with only one crop, however, and all other plant life is destroyed, then only the insects that feed on that crop can survive! Attacking them with insecticides will only compound the problem. First, it poisons the food, soil, and nearby water, eventually ending up inside you and me. Second, it destroys not only the target pest but also many other important animals and insects, some of which might have kept the particular pest in line naturally. When occasional survivors begin to repopulate the land, the pest that thrives on the crop will have the quickest and strongest recovery, making the situation worse than it was to begin with. Finally, these survivors will thenceforward be more resistant to our poisonous onslaughts, and the various problems will only be magnified by further spraying or by more potent spraying.

Meanwhile, the world produces enough grain, vegetables, fruit, and meats to make everyone on earth fat. We have a glut of unsold food looking for buyers. According to a 1986 World Bank study, a mere reallocation of 5.6 percent of the food produced within India itself could alleviate that country's hunger problem.[4] Yet India, and most hungry Third World nations, export millions of tons of food at low prices to the industrial nations of the West, to whom they are helplessly indebted financially. The degradation and cruelty inherent in this situation is only intensified by the fact that much of this indebtedness is for technological commodities that have ruined these nations' agriculture, eradicated their self-sufficiency, and destroyed their health. Nor is such needless suffering merely a Third World problem. Twelve percent of American children are malnourished. Hunger is an ever-present shame for all of us. And it has nothing whatsoever to do with scarcity.

Agricultural chemicals seep underground and contaminate the sources of our drinking water. Directly (through the water itself) as well as indirectly (through the ingestion of contaminated plants and animals) these poisons end up in our bodies. And they are not the only poisons there. Rainwater is poisoned and acidified even before it reaches the ground. Toxic industrial chemicals, sewage, road salt, gasoline, hospital wastes—these are just some of the substances that infect our water. Since many drugs are excreted in urine, these, too, often find their way back to water supplies. In fact, according to John Seymour and Herbert Girardet in *Blueprint For A Green Planet*, "Hormones used in contraception are now reaching detectable levels in some urban rivers. Reduced fertility may result if they are passed on into drinking water."[5] Of course, for much wildlife this water already is drinking water.

Sometimes a poison in a lake or stream ceases to be detectable after a period of time. But it has not necessarily vanished; it may yet be found within the vegetation and animals that the lake supports. Even though the relative concentration may originally have been safely low, it will rise significantly with each step up the food chain. That is, a low concentration of poison, spread out in the water, may lead to a moderate concentration within individual plants as they absorb it over time. As numerous small aquatic animals eat these plants, the concentrations in their bodies become quite significant. A large fish that feeds on many of these creatures will then end up with a high concentration of poison. Finally, when you and I eat two or three of these fish, the public relations experts' assurances of "safe, low water-levels" become meaningless.

In 1978 Congress banned the use of chloroflurorocarbons in aerosol cans – chemicals found to rise into the atmospheric ozone layer, destroying its ability to shield us from cancer-causing radiation. Since that time, however, industrial use of these same chemicals has increased. In 1987, in an extremely hopeful action, twenty-four nations agreed to take steps to reduce chlorofluorocarbon contamination. At this stage, however, reduction will only slow the damage: more still has to be done.

Other dangerous poisons in the air include the carbon dioxide released by industry and car exhaust in amounts that can no longer be properly recycled, due to the loss of wide areas of the earth's rain forests. Tropical rain forests are being cleared at a rate of millions of acres per year for pastureland that is used to feed cattle (a food commodity that the hungry of the earth cannot afford to buy). As we now know all too well, this carbon dioxide acts to hold on to heat in the atmosphere, thus causing an overall global warming – the so-called "greenhouse effect." Because significant rises in planetary temperature might melt excessive amounts of polar ice, an eventual result of this phenomenon could be serious flooding of port cities, as well as the inevitable changes in worldwide patterns of population and agriculture initiated by large-scale changes in climate.

Power stations that burn coal, oil, and gas pour sulfur dioxide into the air at a rate of 100 million tons annually. Automotive exhaust adds millions of tons more, making sulfur dioxide the second most abundant pollutant after radiation. This is the chemical that primarily causes rainwater to become acid. Because it is released from enormously tall smokestacks (which keep the blackening pollution at a comfortable distance from the public's eyes), it is dispersed by the wind over wide ranges. The resulting acid rain destroys trees and other plant life all across the planet and renders lakes and streams uninhabitable, thus breaking the thread of life in two major ways.

Synthetic chemicals, like synthetic drugs, do their work with spectacular power and rapidity. As Rachel Carson was aware, they provide "a giddy sense of power over nature to those who wield them, and as for the long-range and less obvious effects — these are easily brushed aside as the baseless imaginings of pessimists."[6]

Can we survive the violence with which we have learned to deal with anything that inconveniences us? The evidence is in. The food supply is not enhanced by chemicals: it is *threatened* by chemicals. Hunger is not caused by scarcity or by accident, and it will not be relieved by scientific attacks on the delicate balance of nature. Disease, as we have seen, is not being realistically controlled by chemicals: it is all too often brought on by chemicals. And the fruit of all this technological violence against our bodies and our planet is not an increase in general happiness or prosperity. It has led to more poverty and suffering for much of mankind, and to the threat of extinction for all of mankind.

Carson also wrote these words: "We allow the chemical death rain to fall as though there were no alternatives, whereas in fact there are many, and our ingenuity could soon discover many more if given opportunity."[7] Always, when we try to thwart nature, we end up the loser. But when we appreciate and emulate the ways of nature, we often come out ahead. Our technology is unquestionably brilliant, and we have already proven how smart we are. It has not sufficed. What may suffice is a deepened understanding of the principles of natural balance, and a much deepened sense of humility.

The major source of environmental poisoning today comes in the form of radiation. A certain amount of radioactivity, called "background radiation," is intrinsic to the planet. It took billions of years for these emissions to become mild enough for the earth to support life.

Now we have increased the total amount, with the aid of tens of tons of radioactive bomb debris, fallout from nuclear plant leakages, overuse of X-rays, and various accidents of storage and transportation of radioactive wastes.

Radiation attacks us at the basic level of life: the human cell. We do not know precisely what happens when radiation strikes

our chromosomes, but we are aware of several possible consequences. The exposure may be slight enough that the cell can
recover, though repeated doses have cumulative effects that
ultimately make recovery impossible. The cell may be killed
outright—which is why radiation can sometimes be used to
control cancer growth, as long as healthy cells are not also
contaminated. On the other hand, radiation may *initiate* cancer,
though the actual time required for the tumor to manifest itself
may range from hours to decades. Finally, if our reproductive
cells are damaged, the mutation is repeated when the cell divides, and this damage will be passed on by inheritance to all
future generations.

A cell is most vulnerable when it is dividing. Blood cells,
which continually recycle and replenish themselves, are thus
particularly susceptible to damage. This is why leukemia is an
especially prevalent cancer wherever radiation levels are high.
Most grievously, this also means that fetuses, infants, and small
children, whose cells are replicating at enormously fast rates, are
by far the most vulnerable to the death and disease caused by
radiation. Also at high risk are youngsters passing through the
growth spurts of puberty.

America's tragic experience with nuclear power began immediately after the bombing of Nagasaki and Hiroshima, when
thousands of American GI's were sent to Japan for "clean-up"
duties. Military authorities issued repeated assurances that radiation levels were safely low. Many of these GI's have suffered
and died from leukemia, multiple myeloma, and various other
diseases. Many of their children have been born with genetic
deformities. Because these cancers and other serious illnesses
can take many years to develop, and because it is known that
many different factors might theoretically be at fault, it is not
possible to prove beyond doubt that any individual case of illness
was brought on by any one particular incident. For more than
forty years the United States government, as represented by the
Veteran's Administration, has used this as an excuse to refuse
medical benefits to these soldiers and their families. Although
scientific knowledge and statistical studies demonstrate an indisputable correlation between the on-site exposure and the ill-

nesses reported, our government has consistently refused to admit any responsibility for their suffering.[8]

The clean-up activities were only the beginning. Over the following fifteen years, hundreds of nuclear weapons were exploded in atmospheric tests. Because the military wanted to see how soldiers would react in a nuclear war, 300,000 American servicemen were deliberately exposed to these tests. Again, many have undergone lifetimes of pain and illness, deformed children, and early death. Again, in spite of overwhelming evidence, these veterans and their widows and children have been consistently denied any compensation, or even the small satisfaction of having the truth freely admitted by those responsible.

Servicemen were not the only Americans to suffer the consequences of these early nuclear tests. But in the 1950s, few people whose homes were in the Nevada testing vicinity felt any reason to be afraid. The Atomic Energy Commission (the forerunner of today's Nuclear Regulatory Commission) consistently issued comforting assurances of safety, as well as suggestions that support of nuclear tests was a sign of patriotism. But in a secret government conference held at Los Alamos as far back as August 1950, official minutes acknowledged "the probability" that nearby people would receive "a little more radiation than medical authorities say is absolutely safe." And medical authorities now know that even tiny doses are far more dangerous than was then realized.

By the mid-1950s, *leukemia* was a household word in these areas of our country, and schoolchildren were watching their young friends die. In 1965, a study by the U.S. Public Health Service concluded that the regional leukemia rate showed "an apparently excessive number of deaths." But when the AEC protested to President Johnson that this sort of research could "pose potential problems to the commission," the White House shelved the report and blocked any further research. This study—along with many other damaging documents—remained locked in federal vaults for thirteen years. In 1980, however, a congressional subcommittee acknowledged that "the Government's program for monitoring the health effects of the tests was inadequate and, more disturbingly, all evidence suggesting that radiation was having harmful effects, be it on sheep or the people, was not only disregarded but actually suppressed."[9]

A few short decades ago the advent of nuclear power – the harnessing of the bomb's cataclysmic forces for peaceful purposes – was held out as a great boon for mankind. President Eisenhower pledged that "the miraculous inventiveness of man shall not be dedicated to his death, but consecrated to his life." It had been found that enormous amounts of heat were generated in the production of plutonium for bombs, and this heat could be used productively to turn the turbines that generate electricity. The discovery promised America unlimited electrical power at a negligible cost.

But within two years of the opening of the first reactor at Three Mile Island (long before the "accident" at the second reactor), local farmers and other community members began to notice many bizarre things: eggs stopped hatching, birds vanished, cattle could not stand up, greenery wilted, animals were born dead or deformed.

After the accident in the spring of 1979, reports of these occurrences increased dramatically. Pennsylvania's Department of Agriculture (DOA) finally conducted a study. The study took a total of two days. The department reported that only five farmers had complained of any strange occurrences, and concluded that there was "no evidence that would indicate any animal problems in the area that had anything to do with radiation at TMI." Shortly thereafter, a *New York Times* editorial assured us that all the alleged problems had been due to negligence on the part of the farmers themselves, and that the DOA study proved conclusively no harm had been done by the reactor.

But an investigation by Laura Hammel of the *Baltimore News-American* came to very different conclusions. One local resident told the investigating reporter that his family began acting so sickly and sluggish that he "packed up all his belongings and moved to another county." But the DOA report listed him as having "no problems." Another farmer told reporters that he had lost six stillborn calves, after only losing ten calves in over thirty years of farming. The DOA listed him as having no problems. A farmer who lost six sheep to abnormal pregnancies said, "They asked us what we had and we told them." But he, too, was listed as having no problems.[10]

Clearly, the official report had bypassed a great deal. But if these problems were not due to negligent farming practices, if they were in fact due to radioactivity, then why were people not suffering the same fate as the animals? For one thing, people do not eat and breathe at ground level, where radioactive particles settle. People are protected from some of the milder forms of radiation simply by wearing clothing. And people wash their food.

But humans did suffer. Following the Three Mile Island crisis (which I am only citing as a familiar illustrative example, not as an especially unique one), the Nuclear Regulatory Commission, the State of Pennsylvania, and the Metropolitan Edison Company all declared that the amount of radiation released by the accident was negligible and posed no threat to human health. But despite these official assurances, regional infant mortality rates rose significantly during the following months. One local resident summed it all up: "I'm tired of having my children's health used in an experiment."

For the survivors of the original nuclear blast in Hiroshima, death came in five successive waves. Overwhelming destruction of the nervous system brought death to many within hours. Damage to the intestinal tract claimed many more survivors during the first few weeks. For those still living, bone marrow destruction would bring further deaths within two months. The fourth wave began much later: leukemia claimed its victims between ten and twenty-five years after contamination. And as this wave ebbed, the final one began: after twenty-five years, cancers began to appear in survivors' breasts, thyroids, lungs, bones, and intestines.

The message of this experience is that the accidents at Three Mile Island and Chernobyl are still going to be killing people well into the next century.

There are at least fifty thousand nuclear warheads on the planet today, adding up to many thousands of megatons of explosive force. If a one-megaton bomb were to be exploded in the air, the initial radiation would instantly kill people in an area of some six square miles. A large bomb detonated high over the American heartland would produce an electromagnetic pulse that would damage electrical circuitry throughout the United States and much of Canada and Mexico, probably bringing all three economies immediately to their knees. The fireball created by a one-megaton bomb would send out a hot thermal pulse capable of causing second-degree burns in an area of 280 square miles. For a large bomb, the area would be over 2,000 square miles. As the fireball burns, it rises into the air, condensing water and raising tons of debris, creating the characteristic mushroom cloud. The dust and water particles mix with the intensely radioactive particles released by the bomb and then fall back to earth with the wind. A one-megaton groundburst could lethally contaminate over a thousand square miles within a few hours.

All of these effects, plus the massive fires that would ravage vast areas, are immediate "local" effects that could be expected from a single nuclear bomb. But if any of these weapons are ever used, it is likely that many will be used. If only a few thousand bombs go off in a holocaust (a fraction of the fifty thousand that are available), then to the "local" effects must be added the "global" effects. Radioactive debris will circulate throughout the atmosphere and contaminate all areas of the planet for months, years, or decades. Some fission products will continue to emit lethal radiation for millions of years. The millions of tons of dust in the air will cause a darkening and cooling of the earth's atmosphere. Much of the ozone layer will be decimated, and will probably not repair itself for at least three decades.

> Let us consider . . . some of the possible ways in which a person in a targeted country might die. He might be incinerated by a fireball or the thermal pulse. He might be lethally irradiated by the initial nuclear radiation. He might be crushed to death or hurled to his death by the blast wave or its debris. He might be lethally irradiated by the local fallout. He might be burned to death in a firestorm. He might be injured by one or another of these effects and then die of his wounds before he was able to make his way out of the devastated zone in which he found himself. He might die of

starvation, because the economy had collapsed and no food was being grown or delivered, or because existing local crops had been killed by radiation, or because the local ecosystem had been ruined, or because the ecosphere of the earth as a whole was collapsing. He might die of cold, for lack of heat and clothing, or of exposure, for lack of shelter. He might be killed by people seeking food or shelter that he had obtained. He might die of an illness spread in an epidemic. He might be killed by exposure to the sun if he stayed outside too long following serious ozone depletion. Or he might be killed by any combination of these perils.[11]

And yet all such individual deaths would only be "redundant preliminaries, leading up to the extinction of the whole species by a hostile environment."[12] With transportation, communication, and all other parts of the economy destroyed, with the soil, air, and water all contaminated, with disease-breeding dead bodies strewn over the landscape, with survivors screaming and dying painfully, with no medical care, no food supply, and freezing temperatures with no shelter, who among us would even wish to survive? At issue, then, is not just the wholesale slaughter of millions of people during a nuclear conflagration or even immediately afterward. At issue is any human survival whatsoever. It is not simply a question of killing people. It is a question of killing the future. We have become responsible not only for ourselves, not only for our fellow beings, and not only for the planet. We are responsible for all future generations still unborn. All their possibilities, their rights, their hopes, and their very lives are in our hands. We now decide whether they will ever be permitted to be born.

7

Preserving a
Human Future

For all the direness of the situation before us, it is not necessary to throw up our hands in frustration. Global, national, and individual priorities *can* be changed.[1] Actions also can be changed. "It will not be enough that we care," write Lester Browne and Edward Wolfe. "We must also act."[2]

SOCIAL ACTION

Consider what can be done:

The use of dangerous agricultural chemicals can be replaced with biological controls such as natural predators, planting patterns that encourage diversity, and the minimal use of chemicals as an occasional last resort. The goal need not be to eradicate weeds and insects, but to maintain a balance that is both economical and healthy.

Trees can be replanted on a sustainable scale that will provide lumber and fuelwood, prevent erosion of topsoil, and help restore the balance of carbon dioxide in the atmosphere. Simultaneously, carbon and sulfur emissions can be vastly decreased simply by the use of antipollution devices attached to cars and smokestacks.

The energy crisis can be brought under control by conservation, increased efficiency, and a greater reliance on safe, renewable resources. Government regulations, tax incentives, and other public policies can create conditions to promote these three approaches. Companies and private individuals can then carry out the actual needed changes. Efforts to conserve energy have already brought great rewards, as have efforts to increase technological efficiency. And we are at no loss for renewable energy resources. Solar technology has improved considerably and can be used both for heating and for generating electricity. Hydropower from small dams and energy-producing wind turbines are now being used successfully in many countries. Sawdust, animal waste, and crop residues can be burned along with wood. Corn and sugar are being used to make alcohol fuels. Scientists are even finding ways to tap the incredible heat sources deep within the earth. All that is required is that we use these methods in a respectful way, so that nothing is depleted without being replaced; and that we show a farsighted interest in these technologies when oil prices plummet, not just when they rise.

We can maintain the earth's biological diversity by insisting on the preservation of remaining natural habitats and by seeking careful means to restore lakes, forests, and jungles. Much fine work is already being done by conservationists and scientists working in zoos, botanical gardens, and various organizations to reverse the fragmentation of the earth's ecosystem and to avoid a mass extinction of species.

Further toxic waste problems can be minimized with a combination of reduction, recycling, and reusing. Excessive waste is usually a sign of excessive inefficiency, and it needs to be controlled for basic economic reasons even if for no other. We can also direct our scientific ingenuity toward finding raw materials and manufacturing methods that simply do not produce dangerous waste. A tax on the production of poisonous wastes would go far toward encouraging this kind of research. In some cases, one industry's waste can be another's raw material. All that is required is that the various companies be apprised of what is available and be given incentives to find safe ways to use it.

Cleaning up the radioactive and toxic messes that we have already made may well be the most intractable environmental challenge we face. Massive funding and research must be directed toward treatment, disposal, and isolation methods. This critical situation points to the need for a fundamental turn-around in our thinking. "Government regulators often bear the burden of showing that a substance causes unacceptable harm before they can act to restrict or ban it," notes Sandra Postel. "If, instead, industries had to prove substances safe, . . . risks would diminish throughout the chemical cycle."[3] And this would be before years of damage had been done.

PERSONAL ACTION

Much can also be accomplished in the daily lives of individuals. The power of the purse and the power of the ballot, especially when magnified by grassroots organization and a willingness to stand up to pressure, provide individuals with massive power to enact change. From boycotts to letter-writing campaigns to political organizing to civil disobedience, there is no end to the potential power of individual citizens. If it seems hopeless, the cure for hopelessness is to become better informed and to begin to act; for knowledge is power, and action breeds hope.

We can improve the energy situation by employing conservation, and buying only energy-efficient products. We can also find ways to provide portions of our energy needs with safe, renewable technologies. We can separate household wastes and bring them to recycling plants. We can replace most of our chemical cleansers and other household products with safe, natural products, and we can use less of the chemicals that remain. We can decrease the need for preservatives and the excessive pollution caused by freight transport, simply by buying locally. We can insist on simplicity—no overelaborate packaging or useless polluting materials. Finally, we can join and support environmental and antinuclear organizations, make our voices heard politically, set an example, and spread the word to others.

Individuals, communities, and nations have to find ways to achieve survival, health, and prosperity without interfering with the possibility of others to do the same. "Time is of the essence," write Browne and Wolfe. "Species lost cannot be re-created. Soil washed away may take centuries, if not millennia, to replace even with careful husbandry. Once the earth gets warmer there will be no practical way to cool it."[4] But all of these trends can still be reversed. For example, as John Seymour writes, "The emissions that cause acid rain could be completely stopped by fitting appropriate filtering devices to the chimneys of plants and into car exhausts. Every problem has its answer."[5]

The scientific possibility of blowing up the earth now exists, and this possibility will continue to exist as long as the human race continues to exist. We are not being asked whether we wish to live in a world in which the inherent powers of nature can be manipulated for mass destruction. The only thing we are asked is what we want to do now that we live in such a world. We cannot rely on escaping extinction in a fleet of spaceships (as though it were the earth that was threatening us, and not the other way around). Nor does current scientific evidence or any study of history suggest that some magnificent new invention will one day render the warheads harmless: scientific progress has continually increased, never decreased, the destructiveness of warfare. There are only three choices. We can annihilate ourselves; we can continue to live our lives under the influence of constant terror; or we can seek ways to transform the world.

Living under the threat of extinction corrupts and degrades us. It fills our lives with fear, violence, fatalism, and finally apathy. But this is not a one-way street. For there must already be something terribly degraded and corrupt about a civilization that chooses to build, excuse, and rely on nuclear weapons. It is not enough to seek an end to this horror by negotiating new treaties and friendly political agreements with other world powers, although this must necessarily be done. And it is not enough to disarm, although this, too, must be done. To transform the world, we must transform *ourselves*. We must learn how to re-create ourselves into men and women who do not need and could not possibly use the weapons of mass murder. Because in the last analysis, as Schell points out, "it is all of mankind that threatens all of mankind."

Just as there are three forces that must blend together to heal the human body, so there are three necessary steps for healing the planet of its nuclear sickness. All three must be taken simultaneously: disarmament, a change in our social and political conditions, and a change in our own selves.

ACTIVE HEALING: DISARMAMENT

The arms race has been predicated on a theory of deterrence. In effect, we rely on terror to provide safety, and thus, in a certain way, we become terrorists. Unlike earlier justifications for conventional weapons, in which soldiers could and did go forth to defend their homelands, the theory of deterrence promises to do nothing at all for the homeland. All it promises is that if someone annihilates us, we will also annihilate them. It promises revenge, but no victory, no peace, and no justice.

In this system of relentless applications of terror, safety can only be assured by perfect parity: if the Russians do not have as many weapons as we have, they might panic and feel compelled to act before we overwhelm them. Our safety can thus be threatened by an adversary's relative weakness. But the old desire for victory and superiority keeps asserting itself, and we continue to build more weapons, even though the theory of deterrence is totally opposed to this old-fashioned military logic.

A problem that our leaders continually face is that they must find a way to appear "absolutely determined," if pushed, to do something that neither sane logic nor any code of morality could ever possibly justify. That is, they must be able to convince any potential adversary that they are either immoral or insane. Indeed, H. R. Haldeman clearly informs us in his White House memoirs that President Nixon subscribed to this "madman" theory of the presidency.

These are just some of the reasons why we must discard the theory of deterrence. Rather than seeking salvation in the absurd quest for "mutually assured destruction," logic dictates that we create an environment dedicated to mutually assured survival. We therefore must take the active step of disarming the nations of the earth. Otherwise, even with the best of political relationships, we will remain at the mercy of potential misunderstandings, computer error, maliciousness, or insanity. And we condemn ourselves to the absurd task of endlessly planning scenarios for an event that must never be allowed to occur.

Just as we have chosen to make nuclear weapons, we can choose to unmake them. As long as the weapons themselves remain, nothing else we do will be enough. No serious person suggests dismantling all our nuclear weapons while other nations keep theirs. Any attempts to decrease the threat of a holocaust must be reasonable and actualizable, and it will do no good to harbor any sentimental illusions about the goodwill of everyone on earth. But neither must we concede the inevitability of war. Disarmament can succeed if it is gradual and reciprocal.

Considering the redundant capacity for overkill, there would be no great danger in a nation having the courage to take one small de-escalating step within the limits of its security. Such a unilateral initiative would serve to emphasize a sincere intent to reduce tensions. If the other side reciprocates, another small step can be taken. There is a successful historical precedent for such action. In the summer of 1963 President Kennedy announced quite suddenly that the United States was stopping all nuclear tests in the atmosphere. Five days later Premier Khrushchev, praising the American initiative, reciprocated the gesture by ordering a halt in the production of strategic bombers. This tension-reducing experiment proceeded briefly, with several more small successes, and then came to a halt with Kennedy's death. "Peace need not be impracticable," he had said, "and war need not be inevitable. By defining our goal more clearly – and making it seem more manageable and less remote – we can help all people to see it, to draw hope from it, and to move irresistibly towards it."[6]

RECEPTIVE HEALING: CREATING NEW SOCIAL AND POLITICAL CONDITIONS

Disarmament alone, of course, will not be enough, because the possibility that any nation may rearm secretly is always there. The political task at this moment in history is nothing less than to revolutionize global society in such a way that we are able to resolve disputes without resort to violence and war. To do this, we must create conditions among nations and individuals such that the world is no longer so receptive to the threat of war, but becomes receptive to peace.

The chief obstacle to accomplishing this is the entrenched system of national sovereignty. The countries of the earth have quietly ascribed a greater value to national sovereignty than to human life or a human future, and nuclear weapons are primarily built as a means to protect this sovereign status. If any individual country organized its internal affairs like this, giving each citizen the instant ability to kill all the others, "it would be regarded as deranged. But, for some reason, when it comes to organizing the whole world, and providing for its survival, we regard such a system as a masterpiece of prudent statesmanship."[7]

Yet just as we have chosen to live under this system, we can choose to live under a different system. To do so will be unprecedented, difficult, and frightening, but not impossible. While any immediate reorganization of the nations of the earth into a one-world system is far too utopian a goal for us seriously to pursue, we can go ahead with small, realistic steps that will increase international cooperation. Like disarmament, this must be a cautious and gradual affair; and someone must have the courage to take the first step.

Actually, many such initiatives have already begun, and only need strengthening. They include diplomacy, economic incentives, assistance programs, cultural exchanges, and scientific cooperation, especially in connection with global health measures and the exploration of space. Most important, there are international governing bodies that must be supported and taken seriously. The United Nations provides the most obvious example, since it has nearly become a joke of ineffectuality. But, as Donald Keys observes, there is "an ironic circularity to the U.N. dilemma: nations, not believing it can work effectively in their interest, fail to give the U.N. the support it would need to perform its tasks; then they cite its weakness as a reason for their lack of support."[8] As a result, the U.N. has consistently been "undermanned, undermandated, underarmed, and underfinanced." But the purpose of the U.N. was never supposed to be the support of any nation's interests. It was supposed to be a spokesman for mankind. To make it effective, there will have to be a profound change in the way nations view their own importance. In the meantime, so long as a disputing nation can simply choose to dismiss the U.N., it will remain a joke. But the joke is on us.

"The military feelings are too deeply grounded," wrote William James in 1910, "to abdicate their place among our ideals until better substitutes are offered."[9] Indeed, much of militarism cannot be condemned. It preserves ideals of valor, strength, and readiness, while opposing a world of sheep and clerks. These criticisms of pacifism cannot be met by simply reiterating the horror and expense of war. The military mind does not deny these things: it simply claims that war is worth it. It sees the alternative as softness, weakness, and the degeneration of the human spirit. There is plenty of evidence in history to support this point of view.

The solution must be to find a replacement, a genuine test of mettle that will build all the positive character elements that only war has built in the past: discipline, fitness, courage, self-sacrifice, love of honor. Surely there can be other forms of challenge and trial, other motives besides scapegoating. James suggested the motives of correcting poverty, racism, and disease: why not build roads and homes, rather than trenches? "Great indeed is Fear; but it is not, as our military enthusiasts believe and try to make us believe, the only known stimulus for awakening the higher ranges of men's spiritual energies."[10]

Once again, much comes down to education. Our children are taught to worship guns and war heroes, rather than studying the lives of men and women who have courageously struggled for humanity, for God, and for human perfection. Infecting a child's mind with the perverse belief that a psychotic mass-murderer is a figure to be emulated and admired is one of the most powerful precipitants of war.

"Think globally," advised René Dubos, and "act locally." There are many places in our daily lives where we can help bring about a more peaceful world. The best suggestion I have heard is simply that small groups of people get together for an occasional evening or Saturday morning and use their ingenuity to come up with specific things to do. As time goes on, more and more will appear possible. It will also be satisfying and exciting. As Roger Fisher says, "I see no reason to be gloomy about trying to save the world."

CONCILIATORY HEALING:
TRANSFORMING OURSELVES

In the end, however, nothing will change unless *we* change. If we had never wished to harm one another, there would be no nuclear weapons. If we continue to wish harm upon each other, no political negotiations will protect us. The question which each of us must struggle to answer, is why we feel hatred for our own kind and why we are always so close to violence. Then, rather than pretending to transcend this common human condition, we need to find ways to transform it. We need to throw our weight behind our nobler instincts, and to use the energy of our dark side to empower our highest aspirations.

This is the great human quest: how can we unite all the pieces of our inner lives and thus forge a free mind, a free heart, and a free will? The work can only begin with an inner examination, to find out what all these conflicting pieces are up to. It can only be useful if done sincerely, knowing when to be gentle with ourselves and when to be ruthless. And it must be done in reasonable, actualizable steps. Realization of the ancient injunction "Know Thyself" requires long, patient work. This work must be done if we then wish to accomplish the even more difficult step, to change ourselves. But if we do not begin, then we will never become individual men and women worthy of these names. We will continue to be the complacent victims of lunacy and malice. And war will continue to be a vortex that sweeps us into its influence, because there is no unified, conscious self with the strength to resist.

Just as we have unconsciously divided our inner selves into many different conflicting parts, so we have divided humanity the same way. Because of our inner need to feel important, we have divided people into "classes" that nourish our false beliefs about good and bad, superior and inferior, right and wrong. Rather than working on our own inner lack of unity, we turn our attention outward and hate our rivals. We try to convert them, try to talk sense into them, and if all else fails we kill them. Racial, religious, and all other forms of hatred, no matter how subtle, are the deepest roots of war. But if we could all sincerely learn to put ourselves in another person's shoes, to lose ourselves for the moment and consider the total, internal reality of another human being, then there could never be another lynching, there could never be another genocide, there could never be another war.

It is all up to us. Each of us must take it upon ourselves internally to stop reconciling the forces of war and to begin reconciling the forces of peace. Nature has granted each one of us the possibility of cleansing ourselves of hatred and ridding the world of violence and war. It requires that we see ourselves as we are, and transform ourselves into the children of God we ought to be. Throughout human history there have been genuine teachers who have taught us how to do this. Never has it been more urgent that we listen to what they say, for there is already *no such thing as war:* peace or annihilation are the only paths open to us now. Since the bombing of Japan, all attempts to wage war have only resulted in futile skirmishes and stalemates. Many people die but no one wins, nothing is accomplished, nothing whatsoever is gained. This is the peculiar yet wonderful legacy of our time, a legacy we must now make full use of. War is over. We change, or we vanish from the earth.

I am confident that we can change. Somewhere inside us there is a place that is ready to say No to the death and destruction, and Yes to life. That is where true healing begins.

Afterword

It is said that a new age is dawning in the world. There is a growing hope that world peace, inner tranquility, and the universal possession of divine powers will soon be the rule. But I have a final strange secret to reveal: a new age will not "just happen." This may be a time of new possibilities, but there is no guarantee whatsoever that any of them will be realized.

If we are content to believe that it is already our destiny to be swept along into a blissful new era, if we believe that we are already gods, then we will not be alert to any new doors that may open, and we will not be prepared to walk through them if they do. Soon these doors will close, leaving everything exactly as it was.

If there are evil forces in the world, this must surely be their aim. They must surely prefer sheep to real men and women: sheep, who, out of fear, laziness, or sentimentality choose to believe rather than to know, choose to expect rather than to earn, choose to wait rather than to act. Sheep will not take advantage of any new, open door. They will continue to graze contentedly, convinced that they are already all they ought to be, and they will merely be surprised and offended when it all ends with nothing more than empty death.

This is the great danger in all the commotion about a new age. It tells the sheep that they are already real men and women! Two thousand years ago, so the story goes, Christ died so that man might be saved. But man has not been saved. Christ did His part – a door was opened and room was given to follow. But man did not do his part. Man neither learned to receive God with passive surrender, nor to act according to God's teachings for his

174

own salvation. Rather than reconciling his life with love for God and humanity, he reconciled his life with love of comfort. And so, for two thousand years, nothing has changed. Christ did not fail. Man failed. And now we are setting ourselves up to waste another opportunity.

Healing is the necessary preparation for walking through that door into a new life and a new age. Healing means fusing together an open, active mind, a strong, receptive body, and a compassionate, conciliating heart for the extraordinary task of self-transformation and world-transformation. Magical short-cuts, born of the fear of the effort required or the wish to get something for nothing, will not usher in a new millennium. The promise of a new age does not make things easier! It demands tireless effort and tireless love. It is the severest possible threat to our ease and comfort.

We must *create* the new age.

We must take care of our health in order to be useful to ourselves, to each other, and to the world. But satisfying our legitimate needs is not the same thing as gratifying our weaknesses. We need to sacrifice these latter with patience and determination, while we do all we can to heal our mind, heart, and body.

We must gain all the knowledge and understanding we can about our lives and our universe, remembering that the dignity of men and women depends upon our asking "Why?" An ounce of faith is always necessary, but blind belief is the prime quality of sheep.

We must recognize that transformation will not mean simply improving what we are. It will mean re-creating ourselves into something altogether new. Somewhere we must find the strength to "die" to ourselves as we are. But first we must *accept* who we are, and this means we must *know* who we are. No step can be skipped.

We must recognize our responsibilities toward each other and toward the earth. We must not diminish ourselves by acquiescing in the suffering of anyone, or in destructiveness and violence anywhere.

Finally, to heal ourselves and to usher in a new age, we must learn to love God and to love our fellow men and women. This is our tenuous edge of chance whereby the next two thousand years might be different. This is our only path toward fulfilling human destiny. "We must all learn to live together as brothers," said Martin Luther King, "or we will all perish as fools."

Notes and References

Introduction

1. The concept of threefoldedness is found in many places, from the Christian Trinity to the three atomic particles. I first saw it directly applied to human health in Rodney Collins', *The Theory of Celestial Influence* (Boulder, Colo: Shambhala Publications, 1984), pp. 189–98; Collins' book was one of the major inspirations for this one.

2. This sentence is respectfully adapted from Martin Luther King's "Injustice anywhere is a threat to justice everywhere." (Letter from a Birmingham jail.)

1 Modern Diseases Have Their Reasons

1. Selye's conclusions regarding stress are summarized in his popular book *The Stress of Life* (New York: McGraw-Hill, 1956).

2. Walter H. Schmitt, Jr., *Common Glandular Dysfunctions in the General Practice* (Chapel Hill: Applied Kinesiology Study Program, 1981), p. 19.

3. Gary Null, *Natural Living Newsletter* 39, p. 1. Null's newsletter can be ordered through NLN Publications, P.O. Box 849, Madison Square Station, New York, NY 10159.

4. For detailed information on prostaglandins and essential fatty acids, see, for example, A. L. Gittleman, *Beyond Pritikin* (New York: Bantam Books, 1985).

5. Readers can find these and many additional disturbing facts regarding the destruction of the earth's environment by joining and supporting the various organizations committed to protection of our environment (e.g., The Natural Resources Defense Council, Greenpeace, World Research Initiative, etc.) and by reading their many valuable newsletters, periodicals, and books.

2 Confronting the AIDS Epidemic

1. For evidence of a link between the HIV virus and chemical/biological warfare research, see Alan Cantwell, *AIDS and the Doctors of Death* (Los Angeles: Aries Rising Press, 1988) and "The Strecker Memorandum," a videotape by

Robert Strecker, M.D., in which he outlines his evidence that the HIV virus is a man-made combination of two animal viruses, and offers his speculations on why it was made and how it was disseminated. (The video is available from 189 N. Seine Drive, Checktonaga, NY 14227.)

2. For in-depth questioning about the scientific legitimacy of the officially accepted HIV theory, see Peter Duesberg, "Human Immunodeficiency Virus and Acquired Immunodeficiency Syndrome: Correlation But Not Causation," in *Proceeds of the National Academy of Science* 86 (Feb. 1989): 755–64.

3. Quoted in Jon Rappoport, *AIDS Inc.* (Washington, D.C.: Human Energy Press, 1988), p. ix.

4. Quoted in Rappoport, p. 140. Rappoport's work also includes information on the polio vaccine story.

5. Remarks made on 19 February 1988, on the television program "Good Morning, America." Professor Duesberg had been invited to the same show to debate the issues, but his invitation was withdrawn at the last minute.

6. For a thorough exposé of the original AZT trials, read the following articles by investigative reporter John Lauritsen in *The Native:* "AZT on Trial" (10/19/87); "AZT: Iatrogenic Genocide" (3/28/88); "The AZT Front: Part 1: (1/2/89); and "The AZT Front: Part 2" (1/16/89). Copies of these articles can be obtained by mailing $6 to John Lauritsen, 26 St. Mark's Place, New York, NY 10003. Also see Celia Farber, "Sins of Omission: The AZT Scandal," SPIN Magazine (October 1989).

7. Raymond Brown, *AIDS, Cancer and the Medical Establishment* (New York: Robert Speller Publishers, 1986), p. 69.

8. Paul A. Volberding, M.D. and Stephen W. Lagakos, Ph.D. et al., *New England Journal of Medicine,* vol. 322, #14, April 15, 1990, pp. 941–48.

9. "Clinical Trials of Zidovudine [AZT] in HIV Infection," *The Lancet* (26 August 1989), p. 483.

10. Brown, p. 147f.

3 The Healing Arts

1. E. A. Burtt, *The Metaphysical Foundations of Modern Physical Science* (Garden City, N.Y.: Doubleday and Co., 1954), pp. 238–39.

2. Lewis Thomas, *The Youngest Science: Notes of a Medicine Watcher* (New York: Bantam Books, 1983), p. 19.

3. Thomas, p. 22.

4. Thomas, p. 57.

5. Ted Kaptchuk, *The Healing Arts: Exploring the Medical Ways of the World* (New York: Summit Books, 1987).

6. Ashley Montague, *Touching: The Human Significance of the Skin* (New York: Harper and Row, 1971), p. 198.

7. Paul de Kruif, *Microbe Hunters* (San Diego: Harcourt Brace Jovanovich, 1954), p. 326.

8. Kaptchuk, *The Healing Arts,* p. 46.

9. Blaise Pascal, *Pensées* (New York: Penguin Books, 1987), p. 85.

10. Kaptchuk, p. 48.

11. *The Yellow Emperor's Canon of Internal Medicine,* translated by Ilza Veith (Berkeley and Los Angeles: University of California Press, 1949), p. 11.

12. *The Yellow Emperor's Canon,* p. 53.

13. *Yellow Emperor's Canon,* p. 76.

14. Edward Whitmont, *Psyche and Substance: Essays on Homeopathy in the Light of Jungian Psychology* (Berkeley, Calif.: North Atlantic Books, 1980), p. 27.

15. George Vithoulkas, *The Science of Homeopathy* (New York: Grove Press, 1980), p. 72.

16. Lynn Payer, *Medicine and Culture: Varieties of Treatment in the United States, England, West Germany and France* (New York: H. Holt and Co., 1988).

4 Receptive Healing: Taking Good Care of Yourself

1. Information on nutrition, exercise, and stress resistance is, of course, abundant. Much of my information owes a debt of thanks to such colleagues as Walter Schmitt, D.C., George Goodheart, D.C., and Phillip Maffetone, D.C. I have also been influenced by the work of F. M. Alexander, Moshe Feldenkrais, Michael Chekhov's "psychological theater exercises" (which can be found in his book *To The Actor* [New York: Harper and Row, 1985]), and Theresa Bertherat's excellent little book *The Body Has Its Reasons* (new York: Avon Books, 1979).

5 Conciliatory Healing: Mind, Heart, and Spirit

1. Carl Sagan, *The Dragons of Eden: Speculations on the Evolution of Human Intelligence* (New York: Random House, 1977), p. 67.

2. Norman Cousins, *Anatomy of an Illness* (New York: Bantam Books, 1979), p. 62.

3. Bernie Siegel, *Love, Medicine and Miracles* (New York: Harper and Row, 1986), p. 124.

4. Siegel, p. 147.

5. See, for example, Carl O. Simonton, Stephanie Matthews-Simonton, and James Creighton, *Getting Well Again* (New York: Bantam Books, 1984).

6. Siegel, p. 80.

7. Barbara Counter, Ph.D.; personal communication.

8. Simonton et al., *Getting Well Again,* p. 176.

9. Carlos Castaneda, *Journey to Ixtlan* (New York: Washington Square Press, 1972), pp. 236–37.

10. Siegel, p. 181.

11. A beautiful essay on the selflessness and sacredness of love can be found in *On Love,* by A. R. Orage (York Beach, Me.: Samuel Weiser, 1981).

12. The basketball imagery experiment was conducted by psychologist Alan Richardson and is discussed by Michael Gelb in *Body Learning: An Introduction to the Alexander Technique* (New York: H. Holt and Co., 1981), p. 78.

13. Simonton et al., p. 150. Several excellent practical imagery techniques for healing are clearly described here and in Dr. Siegel's book.

14. Siegel, p. 150.

15. Eugene Bewkes et al., *Experience, Reason and Faith* (New York: Harper Brothers, 1940), p. 534.

16. Allan Bloom, *The Closing of the American Mind* (New York: Simon and Schuster, 1987).

17. Bloom, p. 239.

18. Bloom, p. 60.

19. Elisabeth Kübler-Ross, *On Death and Dying* (New York: Macmillan Publishing Co., 1969), p. 5.

20. Kübler-Ross, p. 5.

21. Castaneda, *Journey to Ixtlan*, pp. 81–82.

6 The Present State of Affairs

1. Jonathan Schell, *The Fate of the Earth* (New York: Avon Books, 1982). Harrison Salisbury called this "the most important book of the decade. Perhaps of the century."

2. A. R. Orage, quoted in C. S. Nott, *Teachings of Gurdjieff: A Pupil's Journal* (York Beach, Me.: Samuel Weiser, 1974), p. 207.

3. Rachel Carson, *Silent Spring* (Boston: Houghton Mifflin Co., 1962), p. 6.

4. World Bank, *Poverty and Hunger: Issues and Options for Food Security in Developing Countries* (Washington, D.C., 1986). Also see Frances Moore Lappé, *World Hunger: Twelve Myths* (New York: Grove Press, 1986). Lappé writes that "the way people *think* about hunger is the greatest obstacle to ending it."

5. John Seymour and Herbert Girardet, *Blueprint for a Green Planet: Your Practical Guide to Restoring the World's Environment* (New York: Prentice Hall, 1987), p. 24.

6. Carson, p. 68.

7. Carson, p. 12.

8. The history of America's nuclear power tragedies is well documented in Harvey Wasserman and Norman Solomon, *Killing Our Own: The Disaster of America's Experience with Atomic Radiation* (New York: Delta Publishing Co., 1982). Like Schell's book, this one is not easy to read, but it will open eyes.

9. U.S. Congress, House Committee on Interstate and Foreign Commerce, Subcommittee on Oversight and Investigation, "The Forgotten Guinea Pigs," 96th Congress, 2nd session, Committee Print 96–IFC 53 (August 1980), p. 37.

10. The newspaper stories cited here, from the *New York Times,* are "Three Mile Island: No Health Impact Found," by Jane Brody (4/15/80); "Nuclear Fabulists," editorial (4/18/80), and "Goat Stories from Three Mile Island," editorial (11/23/80). The official findings were questioned by Laura Hammel in "Three Mile Island's Second Accident: How Government Failed," *Baltimore News-American* (20 July 1980).

11. Schell, p. 24.

12. Schell, p. 25.

7 Preserving a Human Future

1. A recommended general reference for the ideas in this chapter is the anthology of useful essays *Securing the Planet: How to Succeed When Threats Are Too Risky and There's Really No Defense,* edited by Don Carlson and Craig Comstock (Los Angeles: Jeremy P. Tarcher, 1986).

2. Lester Browne and Edward Wolfe, "Reclaiming the Future," in Lester Browne et al., *State of the World 1988: A Worldwatch Institute Report on Progress toward a Sustainable Society* (New York: W. W. Norton and Co., 1988), p. 188.

3. Sandra Postel, "Controlling Toxic Chemicals," in *State of the World 1988,* p. 136.

4. Browne and Wolfe, p. 170.

5. Seymour and Girardet, *Blueprint for a Green Planet,* p. 12.

6. From "A Strategy of Peace," speech made before American University (Washington, D.C.), 10 June 1963; reprinted in *Securing the Planet.*

7. Schell, p. 216.

8. Donald Keys, "Peacekeeping Forces," in *Securing the Planet,* p. 103.

9. William James, "The Moral Equivalent of War," in *Securing the Plant,* p. 71.

10. James, p. 83.

Afterword

Many of the ideas in this section – and indeed throughout the book – stem from my modest attempts to begin to understand and apply a few of the ideas of G. I. Gurdjieff and P. D. Ouspensky.

Index